Super Short Stories

Got a minute to be amused, entertained, or challenged?

These 100 stories are super short. None is more than 300 words. You can read one in a flash.

Some are funny. Some are poignant. All are short.

Mark C. Wallfisch

Praise for Mark C. Wallfisch

"You could buy worse books."

- Gertrude Stein

"Mark is America's second best short-story writer."

- O. Henry

"Third best, at best."

- Ernest Hemingway

Super Short Stories

Mark C. Wallfisch

Mark C. Wallfisch

Copyright © 2015-2023 Mark C. Wallfisch

Print ISBN: 979-8-9887405-0-6
Ebook ISBN: 979-8-9887405-1-3

All rights reserved. No part of this publication may be reproduced, stored in a retrieval system, or transmitted in any form or by any means, electronic, mechanical, recording, or otherwise, without the prior written permission of the author.

This book is a work of fiction. Names, characters, events, and dialogue are the product of the author's imagination or are used fictitiously. Any resemblance to actual persons, living or dead, is entirely coincidental.

Printed on acid-free paper.

2023

First Edition

Cover design by Eddie Coffey

Super Short Stories

Contents

Brimming with Style 15

Lemonade on a Plane 17

Finally 19

Broke No More 21

Hitman 23

I Love Going to Funerals 28

Gil 30

Germaphobephilia 32

Domesticity, Roundabout Style 33

Dinner Plans 35

Get Out! 38

Critical Race Theory 41

Callipygian 44

Bell Curve 46

RayeAnne's Wedding Day 47

Dreams Come True Twice a Week 49

Active Shooter 51

Fusion Bistro 53

Steely Blue Eyes	56
I Love You, George Santos	58
I Want to be Alone	61
New Neighbors	63
Lucky	66
"Not Again"	68
Dixie Blues	70
Sally Ladron	73
The Deal of the Art	76
Not Shocked	78
Uber	80
Jimmy	83
Greenery	86
A Gathering	88
Christmas	91
Keep on Truckin'	93
End in Sight	96
Zoom!	99
The Gazer	102
Not Hemingway	104

Felix	106
A Pandemic Mother's Day	108
Storage	111
Dry Goods	113
Cool	116
Thanksgiving Remembered	118
Bed	120
Prison Dialogue	123
The Heist	125
Pedal Go-Kart	128
Annual Treat	130
Hugh's Huge News	133
Big Booty	135
Mother's Day	137
Equality Air	139
Randolph Allen Truetell	142
Matzo	144
Poor Princess	146
Midnight Riders	148
Words with Friends	150

He Makes $20,000 a Year 152

Access Denied 155

In the Garden of Olives 158

News 160

Thanksgiving 162

Dads 164

Speeding 166

A Reporter's Lines 169

Chester's Checks 171

Boredom Relieved 173

Writer's Block 176

English as a Second Language 178

Jet Jalopy 180

Stimulus 182

The Impeccables 184

Insurrection 186

A Party 189

Did He Hear That Right? 191

In the Dark 193

Lecture 196

Arthur's	198
Down	201
One Explanation	203
The Emperor	205
Lady Justice at Work	210
Written in Stone	213
The Gift	215
Hermitage	217
Restem in Pacem	219
Daniel	221
Judging the Passengers	223
No Place to Go	225
Creative Writing	227
Golden	230
Joan	232
Grampa	234
Roger Everson Thackeray, IV	236
Another Mother's Day	238
Slow Burn	240
Courthouse	243

Mark C. Wallfisch

Super Short Stories

Dedicated to

TJG

Mark C. Wallfisch

Super Short Stories

Acknowledgments

Eddie Coffey, Ed Cohn, Jeffery Gregoire, Sharyn Kaplan, Sam Lucero, Johnny Townsend, Sara Wallfisch

Mark C. Wallfisch

Brimming with Style

It was the brim of the hat, snapped smartly down, that gave Marshall that look and feeling. When the wind turned the brim up, as it sometimes did, Marshall swiftly batted it back down.

On a sunny, chilly, windy autumn day, Marshall looked elegant in his C-crown fedora, the classic businessman's hat of decades ago. Marshall wore the fedora with a leather bomber jacket and khakis; it was a swell outfit. He looked and felt confident.

The upturned brim was the Achilles heel of his confidence—with the brim down, he felt like Indiana Jones or Frank Sinatra; with it up, he felt like Lou

Costello or Archie Bunker. Marshall was flummoxed by the wind.

He stood at the street corner fiddling with the brim, snapping it down and holding his head tilted a bit so the wind wouldn't catch the brim. He strode confidently off the curb, not seeing a fabulously restored 1957 red and cream colored Chevrolet Bel Air swiftly approaching his path.

The car tossed Marshall four feet into the air and six feet down the street, where his body landed. Eight feet away, a homeless man picked up the fedora, snapped the brim down smartly, and strode off confidently.

Lemonade on a Plane

As I schlepped my way down the jetway and onto the plane, I curled my right arm around the ancient carry-on, the handle of which had just broken; swung my backpack over my left shoulder; gripped my boarding pass in my left hand; and tentatively held a cup of lemonade in my right hand. Relieved to reach my aisle seat, I tried to get organized by setting everything down in the vacant middle seat, except the lemonade, which slipped out of my hand and fell into my aisle seat. I quickly scooped up the cup and the ice, leaving a puddle of lemonade occupying the space where I was otherwise ready to sit.

"Can you bring me some napkins?" I asked a nearby flight attendant, pointing to the puddle and handing her the cup with the ice. She departed for the galley, and I stood self-consciously in my row facing the sodden seat, waiting for the napkins and letting the other boarding passengers pass by. Those other passengers included a woman followed by a boy about four years old.

As the pair walked past, the boy looked up at me standing awkwardly in front of my seat, and then he spotted the wet seat. He paused, and the woman tugged him along. He darted away from her and back to my row, stared down at the yellow puddle in the seat, and slowly lifted his head so his eyes met mine.

He then turned his head and yelled toward the woman, "Mommy, look! That man has accidents just like me!"

Finally

"Can we please leave at 6:30?" my partner Harvey asked me plaintively.

"That's way too early," I told him. "We'll be hanging around the airport forever."

Harvey, who doesn't understand the concept of getting to an airport too early, pouted. As usual, I gave in.

6:30 came. We put our bags and ourselves into the car, and Harvey drove us toward the airport. He was ready for our flight. I was ready to get a cup of coffee, buy a newspaper, and wait, wait, wait for our flight.

On the way to the airport, we chatted and listened to NPR. As the news came from the radio, a loud blast came from the front of the car. Harvey, his face immediately turning red and his hands gripping the steering wheel, held the car steady. He tried his best to keep us going straight ahead. Harvey put on the emergency flashers and let the car decelerate, and then he gently eased it onto the shoulder. His driver's ed instructor from decades ago would have been proud.

Safely away from traffic, we inspected the damage. The right front tire had blown out.

A Motorist Assistance Patrol truck pulled up behind us with caution lights flashing. Before getting the spare tire, Harvey leaned against the right front fender and grinned. He beamed, he glowed.

"What's wrong with you?" I asked.

Harvey took and released a deep breath, looked at me joyfully, and said, "Thank goodness. All these years I've been leaving early for the airport, and now it's finally paid off."

"Good grief," I thought, "I'll be hearing about this tire before every trip for the rest of my life."

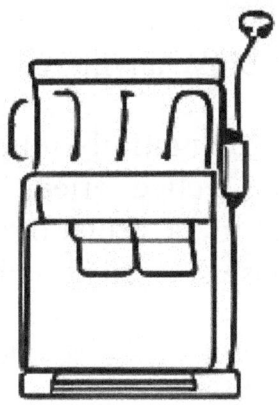

Broke No More

At sixty-two, Grace knew that she would no longer be dead broke. Her Social Security had just started. To celebrate her new, though modest, regular income, Grace hoisted her considerable girth into her Datsun pick-up truck for a drive to the Golden Nugget Casino to invest some of that first Social Security check.

At the casino, Grace lugged herself into a complimentary motorized scooter and headed for the slot machines, where she parked herself, her Camels, and her new cash to gamble for better times. It wasn't long before lights, bells, chimes, and gongs exploded right in front of her.

With seven paylines, she had hit a jackpot of $95,000. She would be easing into Social Security in style, certainly not broke anymore.

Grace was first delightfully relieved and then she whooped, screamed, yelled, cried, laughed, and then she felt the pressure in the center of her chest. She got short of breath; nausea closed in on her.

Grace tumbled out of the scooter onto the floor. She was no longer dead broke, just dead.

Hitman

Gerald made a fortune in hydraulic fracturing, which was rough on the Earth. At home, he was rough on his wife, Cynthia.

One day after a brutal night with Gerald, Cynthia took off her large sunglasses at lunch with her cousin, who gasped, "Did Gerald hit you again? Don't answer; I can tell. Look, Cynthia, you gotta get rid of that bastard. I heard about a guy. They call him a hitman. I got his number. Here. Call him."

Cynthia knew her cousin was right; her anger began to brew. She called the guy. They met.

She told the guy, "I don't give a rat's ass how ya do it, and I don't wanna know. I just want him gone." They agreed on a price and the terms of payment.

Fortunately for Gerald, Cynthia and her cousin hadn't vetted the guy, who, it turned out, was only a former hitman. He had become a more-or-less upstanding citizen, and also a police informant. He snitched.

After her arrest and prosecution, Cynthia had plenty of time in prison to analyze what had gone wrong. Her fellow inmates were generous with their advice. They woulda-shoulda-coulda'd her for months.

After several of those months, Gerald came to the visitors' center at the prison. He brought his children to see their mother. But he couldn't resist taking a peek at Cynthia for himself.

Gerald sat down at the glass across from her and stared into the eyes of his one-time love and would-be assassin. "How ya gettin' along, Cynthia?"

"Gerald, every day I think about somethin' ya said was the reason for your success."

"What's that?"

"You always said, 'If ya want somethin' done right, ya gotta do it yourself.'"

Night Deposit

Big Daddy's Best Burgers, its neon lights brightening the highway running through a quiet town on the edge of the Sierra Nevada, stayed open later than most places in town, 9:00 p.m. Lucki and SueMarie, who were Big Daddy's shift leaders, took turns managing the closing procedures, which included cleaning, closing the register, locking up, and dropping off the day's receipts in the night depository at a bank downtown.

Lucki thought of herself as very lucky, indeed. She could live on cheeseburgers, fries, and shakes. SueMarie couldn't stand the taste of the fatty burgers or the greasy fries.

Big Daddy himself worked only during the day. He wasn't particularly security-conscious given the peaceful setting he had chosen for his burger joint. He patted himself on the back, though, for telling his shift leaders to take the cash to the bank in one of his trademark pink paper Big Daddy's Best Burgers bags.

After switching off the neon lights after 9:00 last Tuesday night, SueMarie drove through the cool air to the bank, where a former Big Daddy's cook held a gun on her in the parking lot while his co-miscreant reached through SueMarie's open car window to grab the pink Big Daddy's bag on the seat next to her. SueMarie jumped out of the car as if to give chase on foot. The culprits drove off as SueMarie, clutching her ATM card, yelled at them through the still night.

Lucki was astounded at the scene as she approached the bank with the day's receipts, observing the agitated SueMarie but also spotting the miscreants' car, which was stopped at the edge of the parking lot, with a grilled chicken sandwich and green salad flying out the window, followed by an empty pink bag.

I Love Going to Funerals

"But I love going to funerals," I told my husband.

"I know, and I've never understood why."

"It's simple. Woody Allen supposedly said something like 90% of life is just showing up. But the way I see it, for funerals, just showing up is 100%. You don't have to say anything deep, or, really, say anything at all. Nodding, smiling, or touching a hand is all you need to do, and just if you want to. You only have to show up to make the friends and relatives feel appreciated, cared for in a difficult time, and all you have to do is dress up just a little and sit through some inflated hogwash about the departed."

"That's it? You're on a mission to make people feel good?"

"Not a bad mission, is it? I might even see some friends of mine and get something good to eat. It's not a bad deal — very little effort in exchange for making others feel loved. I'd go to more if I knew more people."

"But you barely know these people. He was my co-worker, not yours."

"That's just the point. If he had been my co-worker, I'd be expected to go; attendance would be a minimum requirement. I'd be a jerk if I didn't go for my own co-worker; I'd have to go. But this time your co-worker died, so I get to show some love voluntarily. It's a no-brainer."

"OK. You can go with me. But remember that funeral last year? Don't bring up Chuckles the Clown's funeral on the *Mary Tyler Moore Show* like you did then."

Gil

Gil looked out of the airplane window at the gray Texas tarmac. A few hours earlier, he had been asleep. Having awakened, had a good breakfast, and been transported to the airport and screened too thoroughly, he was now waiting, an occupation with which he had become drearily familiar.

Waiting – his life enveloped anxiety and delays. Now he was on board, waiting in the monotony of one more delay for the plane to take him home.

The wait evaporated, as all waits do. This one vanished as the jet rumbled and lumbered and lifted off, with the tarmac vanishing too. Gil mourned as he looked through the window at roads, bridges, buildings, cars, everything in the vastness of Texas shrinking. Dreams are like delays; they also vanish. He mourned. He stifled a sob.

"*Estaremos aterrizando en San Salvador, en dos horas y media.* We'll be landing in San Salvador in two and a half hours," announced the pilot of the flight chartered by Immigration and Customs Enforcement.

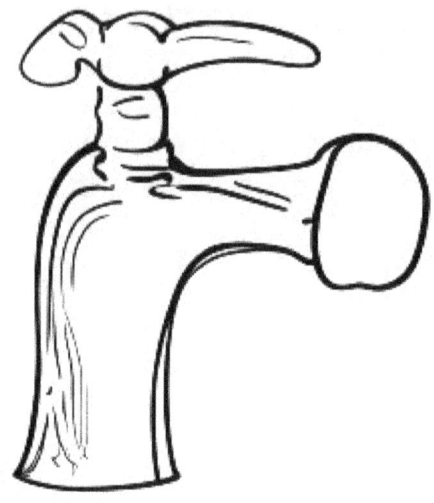

Germaphobephilia

Robert, having washed his hands and fearful of Marie's cold germs, painfully turned the faucet handle by the short nub protruding away from the main part of the handle.

Marie, having washed her hands and fearful of exposing Robert to her cold germs, had moments earlier painfully turned the faucet handle by the short nub protruding away from the main part of the handle.

Domesticity, Roundabout Style

With two other people at home, Grandma Ferdie was trying to watch an old movie on TV while her daughter was at work.

Ferdie's fifteen-year-old granddaughter Angela was modeling various combinations of tank tops and tight shorts. Ferdie's seldom-employed son-in-law Ross, who is Angela's stepfather, was playing a loud video game and drinking beer.

With the three of them in the house together — Ferdie watching TV, young Angela posing in different outfits, and raucous Ross guzzling the brews — Ferdie knew what would come next.

Loosened up by the beer, stepfather Ross would start eyeing stepdaughter Angela and blurting out off-color remarks. That would make it even harder for Ferdie to watch the old movie about a down-on-his-luck nobleman who had to find a way around Italian divorce laws.

Ferdie couldn't stand Ross; she never did like him. So maybe it was time for Ferdie to help the situation along to a convenient ending.

After Ross had several beers, Ferdie spoke quietly to Angela. "Honey, why don't you see if your stepfather can help you pick out an outfit. Take him into your room for a private fitting. Make sure he helps you."

After Angela enticed Ross into her bedroom, Ferdie looked up the phone number for Child Protective Services.

Dinner Plans

"Oh, but I do want to pick you up," Bill protested to Martin on the phone.

Martin replied, "No, I need to finish this thing at the office. Like I said, I'll meet you there. What time's the reservation?"

"7. They said we could have 'our' table," Bill told Martin.

"OK. See you then." Martin tapped End Call.

Bill fidgeted the rest of the day. He was planning to ask Martin to marry him. Two matching titanium rings were in his pocket.

He and Martin were regulars at the restaurant. They had a favorite table. The place was romantic – soft lighting, soft music, a rose on every table.

Bill got there early and sat at "their" table. He ordered a cocktail, which he sipped while keeping his eye on the front door.

Still fidgeting at ten to 7, Bill called Martin. The call went to voice mail, but Bill didn't leave a message.

Five minutes later (he timed it) – same thing.

Then another cocktail, and after five more minutes, same call – got voice mail, left no message.

Now it was after 7 and still no Martin. Bill called again. Same result – got voice mail, left no message.

And again, and again.

At 7:30, Bill did leave a message. He stiffly said only, "Happy Valentine's Day" and hung up.

He left money for his drinks on the table, and he left the restaurant.

A few minutes later, Martin breezed into the restaurant and immediately focused on the empty table with the rose, an empty glass, and cash.

"Now what?" Martin muttered as he gripped the platinum rings that he had bought for him and Bill.

Get Out!

"I've got lots of other things to do," Louis grumbled to Greta, who stood in front of his desk describing her proposal to improve efficiency in the office.

"But this is going to give us all a lot more time to do those other things."

"Only one of us thinks we're having a conversation."

"Louis, let me explain the whole idea."

"Greta, you know if the chief doesn't say anything's wrong, then everything's good."

"Really, Louis, really? Everything's good? Look at . . ."

"When I said I've got other things to do, I thought you knew I meant, 'Get the hell outta my office.'"

"I knew what you meant, Louis. Maybe you really don't want my help, but you should."

"Get out!"

She complied.

A week earlier, Greta had come across the chief at a cocktail party where the cocktails were flowing with no ebb. She presented him with her idea that she said would "immensely efficiencize the office." The chief, about as lit as Greta, told her to run it past Louis.

And that brings us to Greta's returning from Louis's office to her desk to write an email to the chief reporting Louis's underappreciation of her plan. She politely recited her idea, reminded the chief of their recent social tête-à-tête, and woefully recounted her just-ended encounter with Louis. Satisfied with the message, she hit Send.

Moments later, the chief read the email, printed it, and called the head of HR to his office. When she arrived, the chief handed her the printed email. She read it. Eyes wide, she told the chief, "She's got an interesting idea."

"I agree," the chief whispered, "but you know what we need to do."

"Yes, sir. I'll take care of it."

"Too bad," he responded, "I kinda liked her."

Critical Race Theory

A conversation between two neighbors of mine was fascinating. Republican Roger attempted to bait Democratic Dave by saying, "Critical Race Theory. I don't know what the hell it is. But it's gotta be bad."

Dave responded, "I don't know what the hell it is, either, but I think it's probably good."

"Why do you think it's good?" asked Roger.

"Because you think it's bad. Lookit – anything denounced on those whacko news channels you watch, or by any number of idiots or Trump himself, you're against."

"That makes my life simple; those guys are on my side. Not to mention that if you're for it, ipso facto, I'm against it."

"Uh. Admit it, buddy, you're a racist, and at every turn you wanna protect white people from the inevitable trend in this country; we're gettin' darker. So take a breath, and join the future."

But Roger protested, "I'm not gonna let that happen."

Dave lectured him, "Don't be stupid. It's gonna happen, and it's not up to you or some morons who think Trump is some kinda cult leader. We should all be in this together, but you don't think so. You think it's us against them, and you know their numbers are growing, so you Trumpsters are trying to dilute their power by limiting their ability to vote. But we really are in this together, and we should be adults and get along and not keep trying to relive the Civil War."

"I still don't know what Critical Race Theory is," Roger confessed in exhaustion.

"Me neither. But let's agree to live together with all Americans," Dave urged.

"That's easy for you to say."

"No, it's not," Dave continued, "I don't like [air quotes] 'people of color,' either. I'm just trying to be grown-up about the whole thing."

Callipygian

"Callipygian," from the Greek kalli (beautiful) + pyg (rump), means having beautiful buttocks.

Steve was tall, bearded, and a little bit chunky. That last quality included his backside, making it full, sensuous, and voluptuous, rendering Steve callipygian.

He was enticing as he ran in his snug shorts around the park on weekday afternoons, providing a luscious view for those he passed. Some men and women who watched him run into the distance relished the visual delight.

Steve started going to the gym, too. He even started eating right and stopped drinking. He dropped 30 pounds.

Too bad.

Bell Curve

"Look at the bell curve, Boss. That's the normal distribution of intelligence in the population. Half the people are on the left side. They're easy pickins. They'll glom onto simple lies appealing to fear repeated over and over and over. That's half the people right there. Then all you need are a few bigots and a few conservatives on the right side, and you've got a majority."

"Ain't democracy great."

RayeAnne's Wedding Day

It was RayeAnne's big day, and she stopped by to pick up her mother on the way to the church. RayeAnne and her fiancé had planned, and were paying for, everything. They wanted their wedding to be all theirs, every detail theirs.

"Come on, Momma. I left Poppa in the truck. I locked it, but come on. We gotta get goin'. You know I gotta get dressed at the church. I checked off everything, but we gotta get there to make sure everything's right. And, oh, to have a glass of wine just to take the edge off. All these details are killin' me. Ya got your list o' things to check, Momma? Stop dawdlin'. We gotta get goin'."

"You're gettin' me as rattled as you are, RayeAnne. Calm down. We got plenty o' time."

"Not at this rate, Momma. Move it along. OK! Great! You're ready! Let's go."

"Oh, RayeAnne, this is so special, your special day. Ya even have Poppa with ya."

"Yeah. I'm gonna walk down the aisle with him, like I always wanted. Let's go."

They stepped out of the house. But RayeAnne's truck was gone, just gone, not there. She began to yowl. Her mother called 911. A deputy sheriff arrived.

Sobbing, RayeAnne told the deputy, "I thought I locked the truck. I really thought I did. But I musn't 'av'. I can't do it. I can't walk down the aisle by myself. My Poppa always said he'd be with me to walk down the aisle. Oh, please, please help me. My Poppa's ashes are in that truck."

Dreams Come True Twice a Week

Maurice stares blankly at the spinning slot machine reels every Monday and Thursday. Like a song he hums, Maurice is a man of means by no means, and that's why he plays the slots and stares at the reels in a trance.

As they spin, his mind and heart journey into the luxury he'll have when he wins a big jackpot at the casino. He imagines that he'll buy anything he wants. Wealth will make it possible for him to have anything he sees.

For $100, the fantasy of wealth envelops him. Maurice's reality does impose a $100 limit each time he plays. He gets to dream of unlimited possessions every Monday and Thursday because the $100 limit ensures that he'll have some cash to come back.

But, ah, it feels good to emerge from the trance of wealth, having been on a hypnotic, fantastical, imaginary journey. He feels relaxed, refreshed, his head above actual cares that he chooses to dismiss while he's sitting in front of the slot machines. Yes, it is a trance.

When he does emerge and he stands up, he takes an actual journey to the casino buffet, where he surveys the salads and desserts, the meats and vegetables, and the seafood, all with many luxurious varieties at each station. He feels warm and secure. There is no limit to what he can have. There are no restrictions at the casino buffet. For $26.95, fantasy is real.

Active Shooter

"Active shooter! Active shooter!" Thousands of people went running for the mall exits when they heard, and repeated, those words. Adults and children fled, some able-bodied, some mobility-impaired, all fleeing as fast as they could, all yelling, "Active shooter!"

Dozens of people called 911. Almost as fast as the stampede had begun, the city-county-sheriff-police-fire START unit (Shooter/Terrorist Agile Response Team) was on the scene, ushering people away from the mall and searching for the shooter or shooters.

One merchant didn't want to leave. He was still hawking his new line of brightly painted and decorated minibikes. Continuing what he had begun only a few minutes before, he was standing in front of his store shouting, "Attractive Scooters! Attractive Scooters!"

Fusion Bistro

"Come on, it sounds like fun." Margot had read a review of the Fusion Bistro restaurant and asked Benny to join her for dinner.

"Fusion? What kind of food is it? What's the cuisine?" he asked her.

"The review says it's a mash-up of different cuisines. It sounds like you can pretty much get anything you want."

So Benny, a bit skeptical, agreed to go, and he and Margot went out to the Fusion Bistro for dinner.

When they arrived, they were greeted by the proprietor, who was wearing a brightly colored Mexican Jalisco dress. She showed them to a table that had Buddha and Christ the Redeemer sculptures in the center. Their server, wearing a red tai-chi shirt emblazoned with a golden dragon, brought each a menu.

Scanning it, Margot exclaimed, "This is fun. Look, here's corned beef and okra egg rolls. Oh, and here - Mandarin ginger borscht with freshly baked croutons. I like this!"

The proprietor returned to ask if Margot and Benny had any questions. Margot continued her fascination with the menu and asked about the matzo-ball lasagna. The proprietor said that that was one of her favorites, and you can even get it as a side with schnitzel and bacon. "And we have all sorts of green salads with any kind of dressing that you can think of," she said.

"I'm in Heaven," Margot continued, "look here - empanadas with sauerkraut and tomatoes. This is so off the chain!"

Margot couldn't stop reading aloud, and Benny was silent. When the server returned for their orders,

Benny asked him, "Could you ask the chef to just make me a BLT?"

Writing slowly, the server replied, "Uh, I'll ask, but what is that?"

Steely Blue Eyes

This was the day that the graduate students in Criminal Justice learned the significance of the phrase "steely blue eyes." Their professor had arranged for them to visit the state penitentiary, where they were treated to sweet rolls prepared especially for them by inmate bakers; they toured a dismal dormitory, mess hall, hospital, and athletic facility; they were taken through agricultural fields; and they spent a few minutes gawking at the chamber where lethal injections are administered.

Their meeting with a group of selected inmates, trusties, was at the end of the visit. The two factions, the neatly dressed students and the neatly dressed inmates, met in the prison library.

The students asked the inmates about daily life in the prison (consensus answer: it's dull), about access to legal materials (it's scant), about visitation by relatives (it's rare), and whether the inmates had seen Oz, Orange is the New Black, and other popular prison shows (they had).

Then one student asked the inmates, "How many of the five thousand inmates in this prison are guilty?" One blond, muscular, clean-cut inmate with steely blue eyes cleared his throat loudly and said before any other inmate could respond, "I'll answer that."

He continued, solemnly, slowly, and sternly addressing the audience of students gripped by his steely-eyed presence, "Every single one of the five thousand, four-hundred, twenty-three prisoners here is guilty of something." He paused, silently commanding the gaze of each student, and then concluded, "Except me."

Mark C. Wallfisch

I Love You, George Santos

You're my hero, George Santos, or whatever your real name is. You've accomplished so much, not as much as you've claimed, but still at the age of thirty-four, you're a Member of the House of Representatives, where the average age is fifty-nine.

You've got a good job, which hasn't always been the case, even though you claimed otherwise. You're making decent money now, even though the source of your past money, if it actually existed, is still in question.

You represent a portion of New York City and environs, which is inhabited by people known as pretty savvy, though the 2022 election has brought the reputation of your constituents into some justifiable question. But still, they're not hicks.

And you're famous. You're a celebrity. Ask Americans to name three members of Congress, and you'd be on everyone's list.

You're in the news every day, literally every single day. Of course, a while back, so was Ted Bundy, but you haven't killed anybody, not yet, not that we know of. Intelligent journalists beg for your attention, which you share with them sparingly. You're at the top of your game.

Where your game goes from here is anyone's guess. We know that your past is a gold mine of revelations about you, politics, and money. Or maybe your past is just a minefield.

Your present is your opportunity to live up to the potential that you claimed but never realized. As your grandparents must have thought as they escaped the Nazis (if they did), the future is fraught with excitement or maybe just more of the same.

Mark C. Wallfisch

But like I'm saying, the same's not bad. Even though an indictment is now on your resume (or should be), you're a hit! I love you, George Santos.

I Want to be Alone

Larry and Marty entertained themselves during COVID's self-isolation by streaming classic movies. One night, they watched the 1932 Academy Award Best Picture *Grand Hotel*. When Greta Garbo's character said, "I want to be alone," they both howled. It was the perfect maxim for social distancing during the coronavirus pandemic.

So one of them — neither knows which — proposed a game. Each day they would come up with a famous movie quote that was appropriate for pandemic isolation. "I want to be alone" was about as well-suited to the occasion as one could get, but they agreed to search for more.

Over the next few days, they came up with:

"There's no place like home." *The Wizard of Oz*,

"It's alive! It's alive!" *Frankenstein*,

and

"Let my people go." *The Ten Commandments*.

They went onto social media to ask the world for more. Add your comment at:

https://www.supershortstories.com/

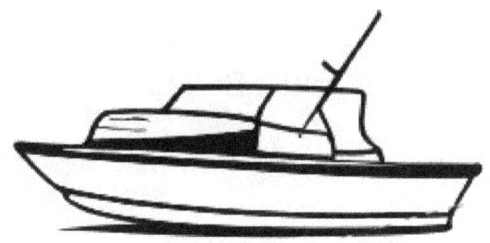

New Neighbors

"Hey, are you guys my new neighbors? I heard two fellas were movin' in," the boater, easing his fishing boat closer to shore, called to Manny and Buddy sitting on the dock of their new house, taking a break from unpacking twenty years of tchotchkes and mementos.

"Yeah," they called back and introduced themselves. Guy Brinkman introduced himself in return and, pointing south, said he lived just two houses down the bayou.

Done. The first social contact of the move.

But who was this Guy Brinkman in the fishing boat? Manny pulled out his phone to Google him.

"Why do you need to know anything about him? Why not just get to know him, you know, like people did before Google?" asked Buddy.

"Aw, I'm just checking him out."

"No, I'm serious," said Buddy. "Let's just ask him over for a beer."

"But what if he's a serial killer?" Manny replied, looking up from his phone. "You know, he could be like Dexter Morgan on TV, killing people and loading garbage bags full of their body parts into the boat to dump in the bay. Maybe he's not fishing at all."

"Ask him yourself. I'll walk over there, invite him for later."

Knocking on the door two houses down, Buddy saw Guy and issued his invitation. Guy accepted.

A couple of hours later, Guy was at Manny and Buddy's front door. "How y'all doin'?"

"Good. Come on in, Guy."

He did come in. He didn't leave for hours.

Manny and Buddy showed Guy around and told him about the diet they had been on. Each had lost 40 pounds.

Guy was grateful for that diet. Dragging the plastic bags filled with their dismembered bodies out to the boat would have been a lot harder without it.

Lucky

Lucky had named himself because that's the way he felt, comfortable financially, related to a few decent, albeit distant, folk, and (here's where Lucky gave so much credit to luck) the sorrows of the deaths of dear ones had largely eluded him.

"Why do you write?" The local morning host asked Lucky, who was on a book tour. It was his newest, his latest, most popular novel. It was all that because it was his only novel.

"I can't tell him the real reason; I don't know the real reason," Lucky thought. "I need to say something about touching people or expressing my own weaknesses or helping other people figure themselves out." Instead, Lucky just stared at the guy.

The host hadn't read the book. Nobody at the television station had read the book. So the host didn't have much to ask. The host jumped into the void with, "Tell us about your book."

That Lucky could do, or should be able to do. But he just started rambling superficially and nervously.

The host cut him off for a commercial. During the break, the host pounced on Lucky. "Strike up the band, bud. I got a story about potty training that can go right into your spot. So bring me some spark of life in the next two minutes, or I'm trading you in for the toilet. Got it?"

After the break came the first question again, "Why do you write?"

"Cuz I don't know a damned thing about potty training. Got any ideas?"

Mark C. Wallfisch

"Not Again"

"Oh, jeez, not again. My life is over." That's what Morty blurted out the second time he was arrested for taking nude photos of young teen girls.

At the sentencing hearing after his first conviction, the judge gave him only a twenty-four-month sentence. She explained that he had never been in trouble before and life events had made him a loser deserving of some pity. In the months before the first time, Morty's apartment had sustained major fire damage (drunk, he had pushed curtains into the flame of a candle), he had lost his job (if "lost" is the right verb for being fired for repeatedly not showing up), and his wife (wise at last) had left him. The judge warned him that he got a break that time but a second conviction would, under state law, bring a mandatory life sentence.

Morty was, indeed, a loser, even though he drove an expensive car (leased for low mileage), looked younger than his fifty-six years (work had been done), and presented himself confidentially as a scout for a modeling agency (he wasn't). But these parentheticals did not keep a second pair of gullible teen girls from falling prey to the car, the youthful appearance, and the model-recruitment shtick. Three years after the first incident, the two new girls went to a park at night with Morty.

He took them behind bushes for nude shots. Was it his stupidity, the thrill, or a need to be punished that kept him from thinking that using a flash at night in the park might not be a good idea?

Patrolling police officers, seeing the flashes, crept through the bushes and seized Morty and the camera. "Oh, jeez, not again. My life is over." Finally Morty got something right.

Dixie Blues

"Hey Earl, you wanna take a road trip? Gonna see Texas, Louisiana, Mississippi, Alabama, Georgia, 'n' Florida."

"When ya goin', Oliver?"

"The tank's full; the trunk's full. We can go today."

"What's in the trunk, Oliver?"

"Oh, a special stash. That's why we're goin'."

"Whatcha got in there?"

"Earl, lemme tell you, I got the beginnin's of a changed United States of America right there in the trunk of my car."

"What is it? Lemme see."

Checking that there was no one around, Oliver revealed a trunk full of cardboard boxes – 100% full.

"What's in them boxes?"

"The winds of change, Earl, the winds of change, direct from our capitalistic communist friends in the People's Republic of China."

"Show me. Whatcha got?"

"This is just the first batch," Oliver said as he opened one box, revealing thousands of 3×4" medium-stock white cards bearing the seals of the CDC and DHS and the title "COVID-19 Vaccination Record Card." The spaces for name, date of birth, vaccine manufacturer, lot number, and date were blank.

"Wait a minute, Oliver, what are we gonna do with those?"

"Change America, Earl. We're gonna secretly spread 'em around for people to take and use on their own. When we go through this batch, I got a friend that's printin' us lots more."

"How's they gonna change America?"

"They're vaccine passports for the Republican idiots who refuse to get vaccinated. Those folks can use 'em to get into restaurants, bars, schools, churches, work, get onto planes, all kinds of places where they can get and spread COVID."

"And why do we want 'em to do that?"

"The idiots'll get the virus and kill each other off. Then everybody else can vote like normal people. The South will rise again, but this time it'll be blue."

Sally Ladron

"I raised you like this? You learned this from me? Was I a bad example? What the hell were you thinking?" Sally Ladron railed at her teenage son after picking him up from the police station where he had been held for burglary.

Sally added, "These are our neighbors! I used to think you were a good kid. We're a respected family. We used to be, anyway. Jeez, what were you thinking?"

"Mom . . ."

"Don't 'Mom' me!" Sally couldn't compose herself long enough to listen to him or to decide on a punishment. She stormed out of the house, leaving for work and leaving her son to wonder what would come next.

Sally tried to relax on the way to work. She thought about things that she was grateful for. She reminded herself that her son really was a good kid, that they were healthy, and that she had a reliable income. Life's pressures didn't negate the positive things.

She felt a little better by the time she arrived at the health insurance company where she evaluates claims. Sally passed through the lobby, rode up to the fourth floor, and opened the door that read, "Dr. Sally Ladron." She sat down behind her desk and checked her inbox, which had dozens of claims for her to evaluate. She started in, making quick work of the claims as she went.

Her supervisor interrupted her after an hour. He came into the office and comfortably settled into the visitor's chair. He smoothly told her, "Sally, you're doing great. I'm not supposed to say this, but the guys upstairs are very impressed with your denial rate. Their pleasure will be reflected in your bonus this year. Thank you, Sally. You're an example for others."

Mark C. Wallfisch

The Deal of the Art

Herb and Blanche were visiting New Orleans when they strolled by a display of painted street scenes hanging on the wrought iron fence at Jackson Square. They paused. A sixtyish, graying gentleman with a goatee and beret sitting in an aluminum lawn chair near the paintings beckoned them.

"Do you like street scenes?" he asked.

"These are good. How much is that one?" replied Blanche, pointing to an impressionistic sunny French Quarter painting that had a price tag of $300.

"Three hundred, but maybe I could let it go for just a bit less. You know, I painted it this spring on Royal Street. I had to work every morning for a week, just to get the light and shading right." Herb and Blanche whispered to each other and said they would have to think about it. The man let them go and remained at his post in the lawn chair.

The next day, Herb and Blanche returned to the street-scene display and stood, staring at the same impressionistic sunny French Quarter painting. They heard a shout-out to them. "I worked on Royal Street in the spring, every day for a week. See how the light and shade go together." Yes, that's what the young woman in a bohemian dress sitting in the aluminum lawn chair said to them.

"Sold!" she exclaimed when Blanche calmly told her, "What the hell, $150."

Mark C. Wallfisch

Not Shocked

Late into a lively party, my friend Gary was winding the stem of an extemporaneous personal travelogue as Maude, the host, joined the guests in the den.

"And Portugal was my favorite," Gary said. "On this particular trip, in the Algarve, I took an apartment with a balcony overlooking the bluest water I've ever seen. It was just lovely, and it kept getting lovelier. One night at dinner, I was startled and star-struck to see a certain Hollywood heartthrob whose sexual orientation we now all know. A mutual friend introduced us. He was truly charming.

"I don't recall whether I invited him to my apartment or he invited himself. No matter. He was there, and we enjoyed the light of a full moon over the North Atlantic."

"This isn't going to get sordid, is it, Gary?" Maude asked.

"I suppose that depends on your definition of 'sordid,'" Gary responded before continuing, "He undressed me so calmly and methodically, and he began to pleasure me, first with his tongue all over my body, and I do mean 'all over' . . ."

"Gary!" interjected Maude.

"Are you shocked, Maude?" Gary asked.

"I am certainly not shocked, but I do wonder why you would talk about such a private moment."

"Oh dear, why else would one have sex with a famous person but to talk about it?"

Uber

I entered "downtown government complex" as the destination in the Uber app and tapped "Confirm," resulting in a newish sedan appearing at the curb outside my home in the predicted eight minutes. The driver was thirty-something, neatly dressed.

"You got business down there?" he asked as I, in suit and tie, settled into the backseat with my briefcase.

I thought, "Good guess, buddy," but said, "Yes. As a matter of fact, I do."

"What you got going on?" he asked.

"Oh, it's just routine, nothing much."

"It must be important cuz you're going down there, right?"

"Maybe so, but still routine, nothing exciting."

"Not like that Supreme Court case that came out today, huh?"

I said to myself, "Oh, I've got a talker here." I said to him, "Yes, that looks like big news."

"I read the majority opinion," he went on, "but I think Kagan's dissent really nailed it."

"I only read a news alert on my phone. I haven't looked any closer."

"I've got a wife and two kids, so it's pretty important to me. You have kids?"

"No. Happy with just a dog."

"Hey, are you a lawyer?" he asked.

"Yes," I told him.

He reached into the center console. Then stretching his right arm back toward me and grinning broadly, he handed me a card and declared, "Me too!"

Jimmy

Four years ago, Jimmy graduated from law school and took a job with the law firm of Woodbury and Nelson.

Two years ago, Jimmy "graduated," as he put it, from the law firm. When pressed by those with an underdeveloped sense of subtlety, Jimmy would say, "We agreed to terminate our employer-employee relationship." The reaction to that phrasing was usually either, "Oh," or "Oh, they fired you." To the latter, Jimmy would respond, "Bingo."

One recent day, Jimmy was back at the office of Woodbury and Nelson visiting friends he had made during his tenure there. Pitching in, he was in the kitchen making coffee when Mr. Woodbury came in for a piece of king cake.

"Jimmy, how are you doing? I'm a little surprised to see you, but how are you? Oh, and what are you doing here?"

"Just helping out, Mr. Woodbury, making some coffee to go with the king cake."

"Wish you had helped out more when we were paying you, Jimmy," replied Mr. Woodbury, adding, "Where are you working now?"

Jimmy froze for a time that seemed endless. He blanked. He couldn't think of the name of the firm where he worked. Mr. Woodbury unnerved him, as he always had.

So Jimmy blabbered in hopes that he could eventually utter the name of the new law firm. "I'm doing insurance defense, almost all personal injury. Depositions are my favorite. All I do is ask people to tell the truth, and they forget which version of their story is the truth. Human nature is amazing, isn't it, Mr. Woodbury?" He was still blanking on the name of the new firm.

"You sure you're working, Jimmy?"

"Yes, sir. I just don't know where."

Greenery

My husband insisted I needed house plants at work. After I reluctantly agreed, he bought lots of plants and placed the botanical abundance around my office. They were everywhere.

I would rather not have had an office that looked like a Rainforest Cafe. But there I was, ensconced amidst greenery beyond my interest to appreciate.

Working late one night, I inadvertently knocked one plant onto the floor. I say it was inadvertent; an inquisitive observer might question that. But never mind the cause. The plant, its soil, and broken pot lay splayed across the carpet.

When the custodian appeared on his regular rounds, I didn't need to point out the remains of the plant. The debris was obvious.

Nevertheless, I told him, "I knocked over a plant. I'm sorry for the mess."

"I'm not sorry," he beamed. "No mess, no job."

A Gathering

Oh, it was a swell gathering, a gathering of swells.

The beachfront mansion opened onto a marble terrace that flowed to a lawn bordered by birds of paradise and hibiscuses and that ended at the wide beach receiving the ocean's waves. The 200 attractive, stylish guests mingled, chatted, and enjoyed the champagne and sumptuous cuisine displayed on tables and bars and passed by the formally attired servers.

As the brilliant orange sun began to set, the servers passed more champagne and asked the guests to gather on the lawn near a platform bedecked in potted miniature magnolia trees sporting the brilliant white flowers of Mississippi, birthplace of Victoria and her mother, Maureen.

The guests talked and laughed as the servers passed more drinks and food. It was a convivial crowd whose chattering was undimmed by the appearance on the platform of a distinguished gentleman solemnly dressed.

Standing next to a silver urn, he spoke into a microphone, "May the memory of Maureen be a blessing," but few heard him. He continued, "The Lord is my Shepherd; I shall not want." Hardly anyone forsook their own chitchat to listen to him.

He continued, "He causes me to lie down in green pastures. He leads me beside still waters." That garnered even less attention.

The gentleman stepped down from the platform and approached Victoria, who was standing at the front of the crowd. He told her, "Though no one is listening, I will continue for Maureen's sake. She deserved that much."

"You do what you must," Victoria told him, "but dear," gesturing her hand around the setting and the swells, "these beautiful people, these glamorous surroundings, this is what my mother deserved."

Christmas

My neighbor Denise told me that a month ago she happened upon an outdoor ceremony downtown for the lighting of a huge Chanukah menorah. She said she met a rabbi there.

Denise asked the rabbi, "So Chanukah's the Jewish Christmas, right?"

The rabbi told Denise that Chanukah celebrates a victory of religious freedom over oppression that happened more than a century before Jesus was born. The rabbi continued, "Religious freedom means that

Jews get to practice their religion and Christians get to practice their religion, too."

The rabbi added, "Chanukah is a minor holiday for Jews, and Christmas is a major holiday for Christians — it's where Christianity started. So, in the spirit of interfaith cooperation, Christians should be inspired by Jews celebrating the religious freedom of Chanukah, and Jews should be inspired by Christians celebrating the birth of their Savior. The two celebrations should be happily separate."

Denise told me that she pulled out of her purse a bumper sticker that she gave to the rabbi, who immediately put it on his car. As the rabbi drove away, Denise whispered, "Dreidel, dreidel, dreidel. Dreidel will I play," as she watched the rabbi's car drive away with the sticker on its bumper declaring, "Keep Christ in Christmas."

Keep on Truckin'

The moment after Rayford's SUV and the 18-wheeler made contact, everyone in the SUV screamed, Rayford braked and got out of the vehicle, and Theresa slid over behind the steering wheel and called 911. Everyone then fell silent while the tractor-trailer driver stopped his truck, got out, and walked toward the SUV.

"What's goin' on?" the truck driver demanded. Theresa calmly told him that she was waiting for the police. Theresa made more phone calls. The truck driver made phone calls, too.

When a police officer arrived, Theresa told him that the 18-wheeler sideswiped her SUV and that her neck hurt. Each passenger complained of something but declined medical attention.

From across the highway, Rayford walked toward the officer, shouting that he was a witness. "Wham! Outta nowhere, that truck driver started to change lanes and, bam, right into this lady's car. I was over there, saw the whole thing."

The officer took names and phone numbers. He then approached the truck driver, who had an iPad in his hand.

"This has been happ'n'in so damn much out here my comp'ny put 360-degree cameras on my rig. I can show you exactly, I mean exactly, what happened."

The officer watched a video on the iPad. It showed the tractor-trailer in its lane, the SUV moving out of its lane to make contact with the tractor-trailer, both vehicles stopping, and Rayford jogging away from the SUV.

Rayford, having seen the video over the officer's shoulder, quietly walked back to the SUV, got in, and screeched off.

While he was hightailing it away from the scene, he made a phone call. "The muh fukahs taped the whole thing! No, not gonna calm down! Now we gotta find some otha sap for you to sue, counselor."

End in Sight

Like happy Chicken Littles, they all shouted about the end of the pandemic. "The end's in sight! The end's in sight!"

Every blogger wrote about the years in isolation and the coming end of the pandemic way of life. Every broadcaster told a similar story, so did print journalists, and social media buzzed. They were probably right; the end of the pandemic was in sight.

Before March 2020, my friend Milo had enjoyed going to work, sitting most of the day in his office, digging through and analyzing data. He consulted with colleagues.

Before March 2020, Milo had enjoyed going to the grocery store, maneuvering the aisles and gawking at all the edibles on display. He had also gone to movies and enjoyed live shows, too.

Then COVID-19 came.

While all of Milo's work data had previously gone to his office electronically, it now went to his home electronically. He met his colleagues electronically, except he didn't need to get dressed or even use deodorant. Sandals, shorts, and a button-down were all he needed for Zoom meetings. Netflix effortlessly substituted for real entertainment.

And deliveries started coming. He could order late at night, and some eager soul would bring groceries to him in the morning. He didn't even need the button-downs for that. Of course, there was anything on Amazon.

Neighbors from a distance, friends on WhatsApp, colleagues on the screen, and fellow congregants at the Zoom synagogue – they all admired his discipline and strict adherence to public health guidelines. Then the end was in sight.

Mark C. Wallfisch

But in the span of two years, Milo had grown accustomed to staying home. It was comfortable and easy. As he saw it, this was not going to be a happy ending.

Zoom!

Dad wanted to attend his condo owners' meeting, but he was in New York and the meeting was in Florida. So I set up Zoom for him, and we practiced logging on.

"Let's do it one more time," I told Dad.

"No, I don't need to. I've got it. Don't assume I'm an idiot," he insisted.

"I'm not assuming anything. I just want you to be able to get into the meeting."

"I'm gonna do it. I'm gonna do it. Don't worry so much."

I thought, if he's not worried, I'm not going to worry. I left for work.

I did, though, set a reminder for myself, and, right before the time of the meeting, I called Dad to see if he had logged on. "Can you see and hear OK?"

"Yeah, yeah, yeah, I'm in," he bristled, "go back to whatever you're doing." So I did.

When I got home from work hours later, Dad was sitting in his recliner next to his computer, with a look of contentment. "I did it, I saw the whole meeting – they're a bunch of nuts – but I saw and heard the whole thing. They even sent everybody a recording of it."

"That's great, Dad. Let's see."

Dad loaded the file, and I watched it.

After the first few minutes, I had to ask, "Dad, you could see lots of people, right?"

"Yeah. Some are unbelievable."

"Do you know they could all see you, too?"

"No, I didn't think about that."

"Yes, they could see you, just like you could see them."

"Oh."

"So, for the next meeting, Dad, please don't floss your teeth or pick your nose."

Mark C. Wallfisch

The Gazer

Keith looks good – twenty-eight, trim, well-defined pecs, neatly trimmed black hair, dark stubble framing his full pink lips. It's a look that gets stares from strangers, and he doesn't take any for granted. He embraces their lingering looks, some playful, some desperate.

He didn't know which it was — playful or desperate — that he saw Saturday night from a limo inching its way through traffic, the occupants on display to the plebeians on the sidewalk. A handsome man, thirty-something, his satin lapels and bow tie visible, turned his head to stare at Keith. The man caught Keith looking at him, and they held each other's stare as the car crept along. The man in the limo gazed. Hardly moving and saying nothing, Keith tacitly encouraged him.

As the limo filled a gap in traffic and sped forward, Keith was quickly out of the gazer's sight and vice versa. Keith had no trouble imagining what he might have said to, or done with, the gazer if the opportunity had presented itself.

Keith did, though, have trouble imagining what the gazer would say to, or do with, the beautiful woman in the ivory V-neck silk taffeta gown and sparkling tulle veil sitting next to the gazer in the limo.

Mark C. Wallfisch

Not Hemingway

Ernest Hemingway is touted as an economical writer. An often-told tale has it that he wrote a brilliant story in just six words. Maybe it's true, maybe not.

My friend Morris, though, is definitely an economical writer. He's a literary miser, hoarding words so they don't get overused. He turns literature into bumper stickers. Or maybe it's the other way around.

Hemingway, you know, was wounded when he was a volunteer ambulance driver in World War I. He was a reporter in the Spanish Civil War and World War II. Hemingway wrote volumes on war, Italy, war, Spain, war, men, and war and war and war. All economically, of course.

Morris was never an ambulance driver or a war correspondent, or even a soldier, sailor or airman. But his brother Nathan served in the Army in Afghanistan. Nathan is stateside now, safe but not sound.

Morris tells Nathan's story in just two lines:

Going to war changed him.

Coming home didn't change him back.

Felix

A gregarious man of Falstaffian proportions and inclinations, Felix hosted a poker game for some of his many friends every Thursday night. He always prepared the same way by putting out wine, beer, spirits, finger sandwiches, deviled eggs, potato salad, and an eleven-layer chocolate Doberge cake that he ordered from New Orleans.

One night a friend brought a platter of crudités, which Felix removed to the kitchen and then discarded. Felix was a creature of habit.

One Thursday night, the festivities ended abruptly when Felix slumped over the table, his head plunging into a heap of Doberge cake. EMTs came to the rescue, cleaning chocolate from Felix's face en route to the hospital, where he found himself in the hands of a talented cardiovascular surgeon, who patched him up.

The doctor prescribed a weight-loss diet for Felix in the hospital and then in a rehab facility. But Felix actually gained weight after surgery, even though facility personnel checked visitors and deliveries to prevent food from outside finding its way to Felix.

"So what's with the weight gain?" the doctor asked Felix.

"I dunno, doc." Felix did not confess that he had made friends with several orderlies who came to his room after hours to play poker. At his request, they brought him desserts that other patients had left on dinner trays.

Felix was indeed a creature of habit. He was a plump old dog, and curbing his consumption would have been a new trick.

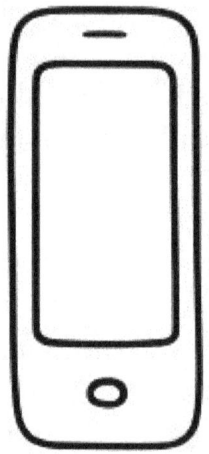

A Pandemic Mother's Day

"Wanna visit Mama on Mother's Day?" Emily texted to her brother Larry.

"Not going out much. But yeah, sure. When is it?"

"This Sunday."

"U got masks?"

"Yep. I can pick u up, too."

"What time?"

"Don't care. Not doin anything."

"Me neither. How bout noon?"

"OK. Lunch?"

"I can get drive-thru. bar b q OK?"

"Yes."

"What u want?"

"Brisket sandwich and cole slaw. I'll bring drinks."

"I'll get it first and be by for u about noon Sunday."

"C u then."

Sunday came. Emily and Larry were both relieved to change out of their stay-at-home outfits. They actually got dressed for Mother's Day. Emily wore a spring-time floral print that she had bought in the winter. Larry wore a starched button-down-collar shirt and pressed chinos.

Emily was on time and texted Larry that she was at his place. He came out. When he opened the car door, he was struck by the aroma of barbecue and by his resistance to leaning over to hug Emily, though he wanted to very much. It would have been like normal times. But he stayed on his side of the car, and they chatted on the way to visit Mama.

As they approached the driveway, Emily's face looked blank. Larry looked ahead. "Oh, shoot!" Emily blurted out, "the cemetery's closed."

In the past, they had picnicked at Mama's grave. This year, they ate in the car outside the cemetery gates, laughing as drops of barbecue sauce fell onto their formerly neat clothes and reminiscing about life with Mama.

Storage

"We store humans 'til they die, however long it takes." Oh, that's not what the ad for Silver Palms Vista Retirement Retreat said. Nor did it say, "We'll take care of your loved one before they rest for good." No, that's not what it said.

Actually, Silver Palms Vista Retirement Retreat is a comprehensive retirement community, offering independent living, assisted living, nursing care, and dementia care. It's like a resort, with activities, shows, meals, lectures, and parties. It's like a cruise that never docks.

Marlene was reading the ad, desperate for someone to relieve her of the responsibility of taking care of her father. She had the next generation to look after, but she was stuck hours every day looking after the last generation. Not to mention that the current generation could use a break now and then.

So she went to see Silver Palms Vista Retirement Retreat, without her father, for a guided tour of what could be her father's next-to-final resting place. It was lovely, just like the ad portrayed. She saw happy, engaged, alert older people in an inviting environment, sharing their last years with others doing the same.

But Marlene's father wasn't a happy, engaged senior. He was a cantankerous, Trump-hugging curmudgeon who had, since Marlene's first day on this earth, been a figurative thumb at the edge of the lens in the photo of Marlene's life.

No, she knew, she was in the wrong place at Silver Palms Vista Retirement Retreat. She needed to find a place that would just store her irascible father 'til he dies, however long it takes. All she needed was storage.

Dry Goods

Abraham and Simon Cohen came to America after the Civil War and found their way to a small town in Avoyelles Parish, Louisiana, many miles from anywhere you've ever heard of. They opened a dry-goods store. They sold fabrics, notions, bedding, housewares, clothing, hats, shoes, and lots of miscellany.

Abe and Simon prospered, and that's how they ran into trouble.

As dusk was setting in one fall evening, Abe and Simon were closing up shop and preparing to go home to their families a short walk away. As they stepped into the street, they saw two worn-out old horses ambling toward them, each with a Ku Klux Klansman perched atop.

The horsemen were draped in white Klan regalia and called out to the Cohens to stop. The Klansmen would have been a lot more intimidating if they had roared down the street with a dozen or so comrades on bustling steeds. But, no, it was a very small town, and this sorry pair was all the Knights of the KKK could mobilize for that evening's mission.

The horsemen pulled up in front of the store, and one yelled, "Hebes!"

Abe responded, "Us?"

"Yes, you! You see any other hebes, yids, kikes around here? Yes, you. You don't belong here. By daylight tomorrow, you'd better be gone. We don't need no hebe store in this town. Now git. Be gone by sunrise."

Abe cleared his throat. "Oh, come on guys, you don't scare us. You've been in our store. We sold you those sheets. You must need some new ones by now. Come back tomorrow; we're having a sale."

The Klansmen conferred and then slowly turned the horses away from the store. One Klansman looked back toward the Cohens and muttered, "OK. See you tomorrow."

Cool

We're gonna crash!

That's what I thought when I woke up on this long flight. Every passenger around me is sleeping, reading, or plugged into some mobile device. Nobody else knows that the plane's angled toward the ground. We're going to crash, and I'm the only one who knows it.

Let them be. If I had the choice, I would certainly rather be watching a movie right now than knowing we're going to crash and I can't do anything about it.

But, oh god, we're headed down. We are really going to crash.

My armpits are gushing sweat, drenching my shirt. I feel throbbing in my ears; it's my heartbeat pounding, pounding, pounding.

Wait. There's a flight attendant; she's walking through the plane calm as can be. Either she knows something I don't or she's the coolest person alive, for now. I talked to her before takeoff. She was cool but not death-defyingly cucumber-cool.

She's coming toward me. She leans down at my row and says to me, "We've begun our descent. Didn't you tell me you've never flown before? So, how was your first flight? How are you doing?"

"Cool as a cucumber."

Mark C. Wallfisch

Thanksgiving Remembered

In 2022, I was thankful for being able to watch the World Cup instead of American football on Thanksgiving Day. Waiting for the Brazil-Serbia match to begin, I could smell the turkey, dressing, peas, and mashed potatoes.

I even took a few moments to be thankful for so many things, so many relationships with people and pets, and so much opportunity. Of course, it's easy to conjure up the negatives — Putin's ravaging Ukraine, Trump's trying to ravage the U.S. by running again, world leaders doing nothing to slow climate change (really, why are they called "leaders"? what are they leading?), COVID + flu + RSV making for public unhealth, inflation taking its toll, and on and on.

But the good far outweighs the bad. We have much to be thankful for. For example, now it's even OK to end a sentence with a preposition.

So, settling in to watch Brazil beat Serbia, I enjoyed the slice of turkey with the mound of dressing, the bright green peas, and the portion of mashed potatoes with butter. Each serving was in a separate compartment of a long-forgotten, three-section aluminum tray embossed with the brand name "Swanson" that I found in my parents' attic.

Bed

Who wouldn't want a $2,000 king-size upholstered bed? The answer, it turns out, is, "Just about everybody."

Sam had such a bed for only a month when Philip, a dancer boy with excruciating good looks and an undeveloped sense of style, moved in, saying, "That bed is too much, much too much, man. It's gotta go."

Wanting to please his new boyfriend, Sam reluctantly set about disposing of the bed. He started with the furniture store where he had bought the bed and where he was buying a new one that was more to Philip's low-brow liking. "We can't sell used furniture," the salesperson said.

"I don't care what you do with it; just remove it, please."

"No, our insurance won't let us." He might as well have said, "No, the pandemic, supply chain; the new normal."

Sam then advertised on craigslist. No takers. He called charities that resell furniture. Each one had reasons why they couldn't take it. One even said yes, they'd take it. But when two guys arrived with a truck, they decided, "Uh, no man, it just wouldn't go in our store."

Philip sneered, "Of course, nobody wants it; it's awful." Sam cringed but agreed to dispose of the bed by whatever means necessary.

Desperate, he called a company named Get Ridda Trash. Yes, they'd take it, for $400. Exhausted, Sam agreed. But he couldn't be home when the trash guy wanted to come. So Sam handed Philip $400 and delegated him to oversee the bed removal.

When Sam got home hours later, the bed and Philip and Philip's things were gone. A note read, "Trash guy was impossible to resist. Thanks for everything, Philip."

Sam smiled and thought, "It cost me $400 and a great bed, but I did get rid of trash."

Prison Dialogue

Inmate 1: Yeah, the skank guard thinks I love her. She's stuck on me, and that's not so bad.

Inmate 2: All that extra stuff from the commissary ain't so bad, but what about somethin' more important?

Inmate 1: Like what?

Inmate 2: Come on! She's got the keys to the place. She can get us both outta here.

Inmate 1: Us?

Inmate 2: You love birds wouldn't leave me behind, would ya?

Inmate 1: Did Meghan and Harry take Andrew with them?

Inmate 2: Ain't the same thing.

Inmate 1: Maybe not, but her gettin' both of us out is gonna be a little tricky. Just gettin' me out is gonna be tricky enough.

Inmate 2: Yeah, and she'll be leadin' you around by the ring in your nose, just like Meghan and Harry. It's prison one way or another.

The Heist

After seeing the homeowner, who was driving a Mercedes GLE coupe, leave a classic mid-century modern home, my friend Carter snuck into the home's backyard and entered the house through a window that had been left ajar. Walking through the residence, Carter casually surveyed the contents looking for good gear to grab. In one bedroom, he found a Tag Heuer Formula 1 watch and an onyx ring, both easy to slip into his jeans and easy to fence. In another bedroom, he found $120 in cash; "perfect," he whispered to himself. Then he saw shoes on the floor.

His eyes grew big as he examined the purple Versace sneakers, a model he had long coveted. His eyes danced when he saw that they were 10's, his size. Carter slipped them on, enjoying the look and feel. He nestled his well-worn Walmart sneakers under his left arm and, ecstatic with his haul, climbed out the back window and tossed his own shoes into a nearby construction dumpster. He sauntered home.

In his elation over the success of the heist, Carter had not noticed that a neighbor of the homeowner saw him climb out the window. She called 911. The police later found Carter, and a trial ensued.

The prosecutor had scheduled two witnesses. First was the homeowner, a portion of whose testimony is reproduced below. Second was the neighbor, whose testimony turned out to be superfluous.

Transcript

Prosecutor: Describe for the jury the items that were missing.

Homeowner: A Tag Heuer Formula 1 watch, an onyx ring, and $120 in cash.

Prosecutor: Anything else?

Homeowner: Yes. Sneakers.

Prosecutor: Can you describe the sneakers?

Homeowner: No need to. [Pointing to the defendant] They're the purple Versace sneakers that that guy is wearing right now.

Defense attorney: Oh crap.

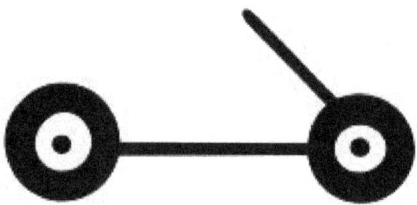

Pedal Go-Kart

Sebastian, in fair shape at forty-six, daily walked clockwise a few times around the one-mile path surrounding a neighborhood lake. On a recent day, a twenty-something-year-old man was at the lake pedaling a go-kart counter-clockwise along the same path. The young man exclaimed, "Looking good!" as he passed Sebastian.

The words "looking good" floated in Sebastian's head as did the image of the handsome pedaler's sweaty thighs glimmering in the bright summer sun. At least a couple of decades older than the pedaler,

Sebastian was feeling good even if maybe not, as in the pedaler's words, looking good.

On the next pass around the lake, the pedaler said, "Later," and cruised by. The word "later" and the sweat dripping off the young man's thighs flustered Sebastian, who still hadn't said anything. Sebastian's brain was occupied by the anticipation of another meeting as they continued to circle the lake in opposite directions.

Anxiously trying to think of something to say, Sebastian was unprepared when he saw the go-kart coming his way again. Sebastian awkwardly blurted out, "Sure, later," as the go-kart rolled by. The younger man slowed, turned his head to look back at Sebastian and said, "Hold on. Huh?"

With the pedaler's head turned back toward the older man, the sweaty thighs weren't directly in Sebastian's gaze. Sebastian's focus instead was on the young man's quizzical look and the Bluetooth earpiece in the young man's ear.

Mark C. Wallfisch

Annual Treat

It's called a "blanket" of snow because it covers everything; it's comforting, you feel secure. That's what there was on this quiet morning with no traffic and no activity in the street. It was beautiful, even though it would be a mess to drive in. In the early hours, lights were still twinkling up and down the street. Inflatable characters and decorations were still puffed up with joy. There was Santa, lots of Santas, thousands of lights, crèches, dinosaur reindeer, and a wooden troupe of Elvis elves.

Adam and Rebecca looked out the front window as the kids came screeching down the stairs into the living room. They wanted to leave right then, ready for their annual treat. Adam had to calm them down, or he tried to. He told them that breakfast comes first, but that was just foolishness to the kids.

Rebecca tempted them with Lucky Charms. That calmed them a bit, but just a bit. They left most of it untouched.

"When are we going to go?" the children demanded.

"Not yet, not until noon," Adam told them.

"We're ready now, now, now," they countered.

"No," Adam said, "we still have to wait, but we can get a head start. Let's look at the menu online."

They all crowded around Adam's desk to look at a restaurant menu on his computer screen.

"OK," Adam said, addressing the three kids, "who wants what?"

"I want egg rolls," shouted one child.

"I want fried rice," added another one.

"I want cashew chicken," said the third.

Adam, smiling, turned to Rebecca and said, "Oh, its going to be a happy Christmas Day for us Bernsteins."

Hugh's Huge News

Hugh bounded through the front door of the gracious suburban home he shared with his wife, Delores. Hugh bellowed, "Honey, I bought a new house!"

"You what?" Delores exclaimed.

"And you'll love it. You know I like change. You'll like the new house, too. It's near the club, shopping, and lots of friends. And it's got a pool. You've always wanted a pool."

"This is so typical! You like change, so we move. But what about me?"

"No 'but's. It'll be a great change. I know you'll adore it. We need to start packing."

Hugh eased into a living room chair with a whiskey, neat, while Delores went upstairs. She returned to the living room twenty minutes later with two suitcases.

"Just two suitcases, that's all you're packing?" Hugh asked.

"Yes, dear. I like change, too."

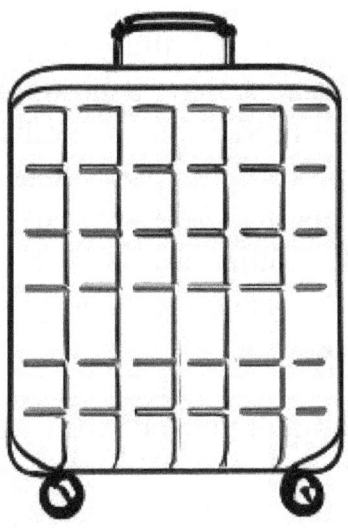

Big Booty

Orson and Arthur fly First or Business Class because they're tall guys. Coach is just too cramped. So there was no question that they'd fly Business Class to Santiago de Chile on their way to Patagonia to board a cruise ship.

Easing into their roomy airline seats with lots of legroom, Orson kicked off his well-worn size 13 Gucci leather sneakers and Arthur kicked off his size 12 Louis Vuitton loafers. They drank cocktails, dined, and browsed articles about Chile.

They read myths about Chile, too. There was one about a mermaid with golden hair who comes ashore in southern Chile to predict the size of the fish harvest. But she doesn't really come ashore, and, if she does, she doesn't make predictions. Another one tells that some early explorers reported that the people of Patagonia are giants. They're not; they're rather diminutive. Still another one has it that, on one island, a wood troll impregnates teenage girls. He doesn't; their boyfriends do.

After the flight, Orson and Arthur had a marvelous time in Santiago and then Punta Arenas in Patagonia, touring museums, churches, and parks. They dined on empanadas, barbecue, stews, abundant seafood, and, of course, Chilean wine. The night before the cruise, they turned their luggage over to the cruise company and turned into bed at their hotel.

The next day they were startled at being advised by the captain of the ship that their luggage had been stolen. "Oh no!" Orson exclaimed, "What are we going to do for clothes?"

About the same time, the Patagonian thieves opened the guys' suitcases to examine their haul. Holding up Orson's brand-new size 13 Gucci boots, one small-framed thief exclaimed, *"¡Oh no! ¡Trastos inútiles!"* Oh no! Useless junk!

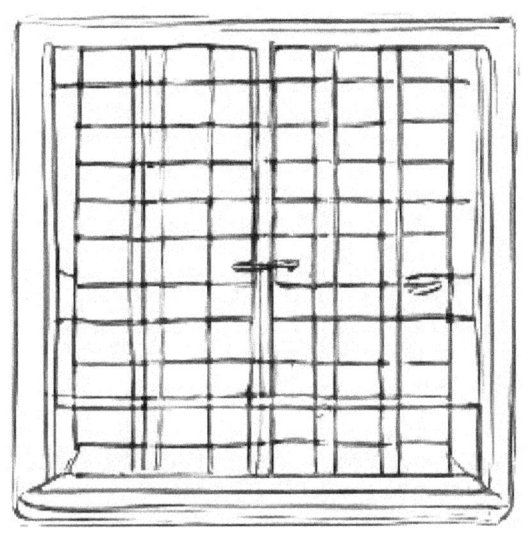

Mother's Day

"Oh, Ma, I'm so glad to see ya," Buster said to his mother, Agnes.

"And on Mother's Day, too, Buster. Prison's an awful place, especially when there wan'n all that much wrong wit . . ."

"Don't re-live that, Ma, not again. Let's make it a happy Mother's Day, as happy as we can, anyway."

"OK. You're right. So, whatcha been doin', Buster?"

"Got a hospital job – orderly. Ain't pretty, pays just a little, but keeps me busy and outta trouble."

"Good, son, this family don't need no more trouble."

"How 'bout you, Ma, whatcha doin'?"

"Didn't I tell ya? I'm takin' an art class. Got a great teacher. I'm workin' wit acrylics, just startin' to get a real feel for it."

"That's great, Ma. Got anything you can show me?"

"Not yet, Buster, not ready yet. When I do, they'll post somethin' for you to see."

"Great, Ma. And maybe next time . . ."

"Time's up! Mother's Day's over," shouted a correctional officer. "Back to your cellblock, Agnes. Your son's gotta leave now."

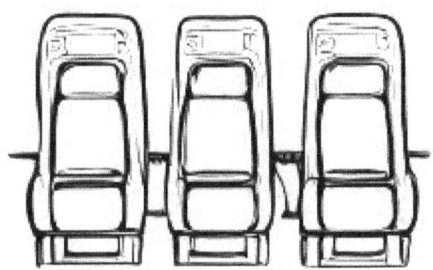

Equality Air

The perky young woman sitting next to me in the Economy cabin whispered to me, "I always try to toot my horn when I walk through First Class."

"Excuse me. You what?"

"Try to toot my horn."

I looked at her blankly.

"You know, let a breeze out the back door, play the o-ring oboe, release a squeaker . . ."

"You do what?"

"Break wind, pass gas . . ."

"Oh," I half-smiled, never before having heard a confession to one's intentional flatulence while walking past the more privileged passengers.

She gave me a devilish wink, enticing me into making this a conversation.

I cautiously complied, responding, "How'd you do today? I mean, were you successful? Did you let one loose?"

"Oh, god, yes, I even feel a little sorry for the poor shlubs who were walking behind me."

"Those poor shlubs," I said, "were just passing through while you were passing gas. But the people actually sitting up there were trapped in your gas chamber."

"Not my chamber. It's theirs, bought (or rented) and paid for; they paid way more for their seats than we did for ours."

"Is this class warfare?"

"Of course, but I'm only a pawn. The kings and queens started it. I didn't divide the plane into classes. I only expressed my opinion about it. Really expressed my opinion."

It didn't take any more than those few lines for our conversation to run its course, and so the imaginative discussion of flatulence-based Marxism never found its full voice. Oh, and I didn't tell my seat neighbor that, earlier that day, I had had a huge plate of beans for lunch. Economy and First Class were about to become much more equal.

Mark C. Wallfisch

Randolph Allen Truetell

The parents loved Randolph Allen Truetell, school principal. The kids loved him too.

Then the word began to spread: Randy didn't have a doctorate like he said. He didn't have a master's degree, either. He wasn't even a college graduate.

Randy was pressured to resign. It was all over the news. The church where he preached—he falsified a divinity degree, too—let him go. He was ridiculed and laughed at, especially given his last name and initials.

Randy didn't understand that habitual or compulsive lying is the product of low self-esteem. Nor did he know that low self-esteem and depression often go together.

Before the truth came out, the respect and love he got at school and church soothed his low self-esteem and rid him of signs of depression. He had actually been faking it all very well. But his functioning evaporated with his careers. Depression embraced him, or vice versa.

So he sought the help of a psychologist, who listened to him patiently and compassionately. The psychologist told him he needed to pick himself up, dust himself off, and go on with his life.

Randy did go on, but only as far as to attempt suicide.

The psychologist didn't even visit Randy in the hospital. But the psychologist had an excuse; he was busy fighting charges that he had plagiarized his doctoral dissertation.

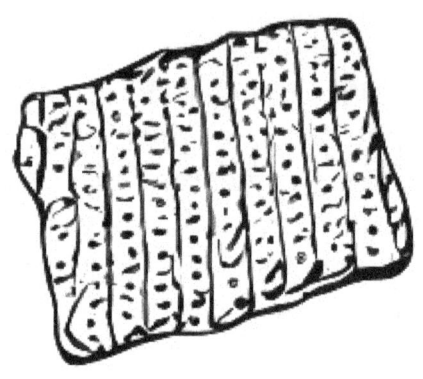

Matzo

"Can't you do anything right?" Sammy sneered at Molly when he saw her stacking the matzos without placing one in between layers of cloth as prescribed by generations of tradition. Matzo, known as the bread of affliction, is the centerpiece of the Passover Seder. In Sammy's view, his wife was screwing up their first Seder together.

Sammy is from a family more anchored in Jewish tradition than Molly's. "From," actually is the wrong word. Sammy is still very much a part of that family.

He hasn't gone "from" it. He carries them and their inflexible adherence to tradition with him.

Molly didn't deserve a disdainful rebuke. She paused to wonder how she could have made herself so ignorant of Sammy's weaknesses while they were dating and then engaged. All the times that she had made excuses for his judgmental b.s. suddenly came into focus in that one moment about matzo that was both tragic and liberating. It was tragic because it was devastating and demoralizing. It was liberating because she determined in that brief moment that her first Seder with Sammy would be her last. Sammy was Pharaoh, Molly the Jews.

The Seder came and went. Sammy behaved himself, more or less, during the dinner. The stinging rebuke was no longer in his consciousness and was certainly never in his conscience.

Cleaning up after Seder, though, was as tense as the preparation, though the glow of her impending liberation shone through for Molly. As the dishwasher whirred, Sammy and Molly, exhausted, fell onto two distinct sides of their king size mattress atop their bed of affliction.

Mark C. Wallfisch

Poor Princess

My neighbor Harold soberly told me that he couldn't afford pricey surgery for his dog Princess. "June loves that dog, but we're going to have to put her down . . . Poor Princess," Harold sniffled, but just a little bit. He didn't produce any tears. He said it matter of factly. He couldn't afford the operation. He made it seem simple.

If he couldn't afford it, he couldn't afford it, I thought at first. Like the Pope said, "Who am I to judge?"

Fortunately, I don't have to meet papal standards for empathy. I judged.

Harold can't afford the dog's surgery, but he drives a new Lexus, has season Saints tickets, and eats dinners at Ruth's Chris? Poor Princess, indeed. I hrrumphed to myself. I gave Harold my faux sympathy for his impending loss.

"Anyway, in time, I'll get June another dog; she'll be OK," Harold added as he left.

June came by the next day, looking exhausted. "I just got back from the hospital," she told me. "Princess escaped from the house. Harold chased after her, and he collapsed in the street. The doctor says he needs surgery. I just don't know how we're going to afford it . . . Poor Harold."

Mark C. Wallfisch

Midnight Riders

After January 6, 2021, the FBI went through my neighbor Jeremy's emails and texts. They found the following exchange and others between Jeremy and someone named Myron, who lived about 200 miles away.

Jeremy: You know about Paul Revere, right? They say he was booted and spurred, with a heavy stride, ready to ride to make America free. Like back then, the enemies of freedom are after us now. Keep your boots and your spurs ready cuz we gotta ride again.

Myron: Hold on. Didn't we let ourselves get swept up in a crazy time when we met in DC back in January? Paul Revere wasn't sucked in by a lame duck with a smashed ego.

Jeremy: No, we got a country to save.

Myron: Right about that. The country needs saving, but it's not from your demons. I love you, but that Paul Revere part is a little scary.

Jeremy: Then why'd you go to DC?

Myron: At first, it seemed like an important thing to do. And I wanted to meet hot guys, hot like you.

Jeremy: Yeah, that was a great night. Let's do that again.

Myron: Yeah, but without all that fate-of-a-nation stuff. The nation's fine if we just don't ride into darkness.

Jeremy: But I still want to hold you tight in bed, smelling your sweat. I really am on Paul Revere's ride for you.

Myron: Oh geez. Just drive over here this weekend. We'll binge watch something that's not political, eat pizza, and who knows what else.

Mark C. Wallfisch

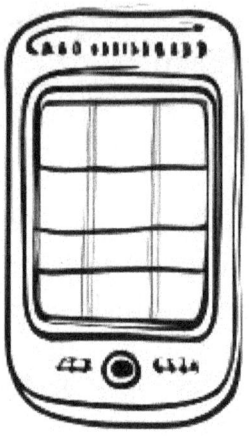

Words with Friends

Carl's wife says it's an addiction. Carl's children say it's an obsession. Carl says it's just a game. It's a game called Words with Friends that Carl plays incessantly on his phone. It's similar to Scrabble.

During a recent match, Carl muttered, "I'm not going to let that bastard beat me again." Carl tried to figure out how to get a triple word score to solidify his lead against his long-time rival. Carl detests losing, especially to his archenemy. Letting that creep defeat him turns Carl inside out.

"Now where to put that damned 'Z'?" Carl continued muttering. He had all consonants, including a "Z." "I've got nothing, nothing, nothing!" Carl was about to explode.

"Wait, I can put the 'Z' next to . . . Crap!" Carl screamed as his SUV rear-ended the truck ahead of him and the airbag exploded out of his steering wheel.

Mark C. Wallfisch

He Makes $20,000 a Year

There are quotations on the wall at work.

"Life's most persistent and urgent question is, 'What are you doing for others?'" Dr. Martin Luther King, Jr.

"Ask not what your country can do for you — ask what you can do for your country." President John F. Kennedy.

"The reward of a thing well done is to have done it." Ralph Waldo Emerson

Mack makes $20,000 a year. Dr. King, President Kennedy, Ralph Whoever – they don't much interest him. Not that he feels anything ill about them; he just doesn't feel much about them at all. Their inspirational quotations do not inspire him.

He likes the job. It gives Mack a day with structure and something to do. If the bosses wanted to put a quotation of Mack's on the wall, it could be, "I do something."

One Friday, a coworker asked Mack if he had any special plans for the biweekly paycheck that had been direct deposited that day. Surprised by the question, Mack uttered casually, "Oh, is today payday?"

Another coworker, Brian, pulled Mack aside and whispered, "Don't let people think you don't know it's payday."

"Oh, right, gotcha, OK," Mack replied.

Brian, who knew that Mack's late parents had provided well for him, asked, "Why on earth do you work anyway, Mack? This place can't mean much to you, does it?"

"It doesn't mean much to me, not anything grand like those guys on the wall say. But it means a lot to me – a place for me to come every day. Where else do I get that?"

Access Denied

"I dunno," Leo said when the officer asked him who Marcus Trumbley was.

"His name's on the credit card you were tryin' to use, but you don't know who he is?"

"He's a friend."

"He gave you this card?"

"Yeah, I don't wanna talk. Are you arrestin' me?"

"Not right now, but we need to find out how you got this card."

"Like I said, I got nuthin to say."

Leo is a coroner's assistant who transports cadavers to the coroner's office. He often picks up fully-clothed bodies that have pockets with items worth taking. He also goes into houses, into rooms where he's alone with corpses, no one there to see when he removes more than the bodies. The officer didn't know yet that he would find at Leo's home other credit cards that Leo had taken from the departed.

The law calls credit cards "access devices," which is an apt term for cards that are keys to commerce, until there's an illegal scheme and access is denied. During a trip to Walmart, Leo's access had been denied.

"So how'd you get Marcus Trumbley's card?" the officer persisted. After a lot of hemming and hawing, Leo admitted that he stole from the dead.

"What are you tryin' to pull here?" the officer asked hours later. "The coroner says he's had no cadaver named Marcus Trumbley. Plus we found other cards at your apartment – all in names the coroner doesn't have record of. Where you been gettin' these cards?"

"Honest, only from stiffs. This must be entrapment. You musta planted cards for me to find."

"No, you're just robbin' the wrong kinda dead people. You're robbin' thieves, dead thieves," the officer eventually figured out.

"Hell, ya can't trust nobody, and I mean 'no body,'" Leo figured out.

In the Garden of Olives

Rabbi Nate Rosenberg and Rev. Lou Warren had known each other for years through an ecumenical clergy group in Fort Lauderdale. When Rev. Lou asked Rabbi Nate to meet him for lunch at the mall, Nate agreed.

They met and small-talked over breadsticks, salad, lasagna classico and chicken parmigiana, and, after they had eaten, Lou took a deep breath and reached for Nate's hand.

"What's going on?" Nate thought.

Looking into Nate's startled eyes, Lou piously intoned, "Nate, isn't it time for you to come with me to Jesus, and together we can lead your people to the one true Savior?"

Nate's incredulity of a moment ago diminished in comparison to the astonishment now in Nate's mind. It took what felt like hours for him to proceed through resentment and anger to compose himself to respond.

Sitting erect and pushing back from the table, Nate replied intently, "Lou, I love living in this town. I've met so many great people. The beaches are beautiful, and the history is fascinating. The tropical weather is so relaxing. I enjoy splurging on dinners at Morton's, the Lobster Bar Sea Grille, Casa D'Angelo, and other fabulous restaurants.

"But Lou, if I'm reading you right, you're asking me to turn my back on 6000 years of Jewish history at — of all places — Olive Garden?"

News

Todd had long been fascinated by news stories of patricide and matricide, the TV and YouTube reports getting most of his attention. He also had a cache of newspaper and magazine articles from years ago about children killing their parents. Unfortunately for Todd, all of the dramas ended poorly for the perpetrators with life or death sentences.

When his parents retired at the start of the pandemic after working forty years and sold their regional chain of jewelry stores to a national chain, the pot-of-jewelry gold that one day might be his weighed heavily on Todd's mind. He went back through the print and online slaughter sagas to look for a way to avoid the state criminal justice system, which could stand between him and the pot of gold.

Todd monitored established news outlets and online sources of information and misinformation for inspiring ways to get his hands into the pot of gold. A recent plunge in stock prices made him worry momentarily about the bounty in the pot, but he was confident that his parents had wisely diversified their assets.

Todd was not a panicker. He was too thoughtful for that, and his thoughtfulness turned to his parents' golden wedding anniversary coming up soon. He stuffed into an elegant, golden gift bag many booklets, brochures, pictures, and pages of information about the around-the-world cruise he was sending them on for their anniversary.

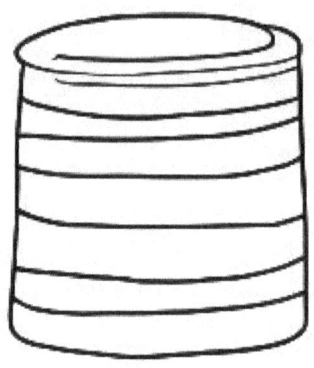

Thanksgiving

"Yes, my mother made it like that, and, in fact, her mother did, too," Les told Michael.

"So it's time for the madness to stop, right?" Michael replied.

"I'll add a second vegetable dish — anything you want — but we definitely have to have the casserole with canned green beans and cream of mushroom soup," Les countered.

"OK. I got it. But how about some real cranberries this year?" Michael asked.

Les's eyes widened, and he said, "Oh, I love those little ridges. They really mean Thanksgiving to me. I'll make a recipe I heard on NPR, too, but we've got to have the red cylinder with those ridges."

When the guests had been invited and the menu set, Michael and Les were ready to get ready for Thanksgiving. Michael did the grocery shopping.

At Kroger, while buying the items that Les had specified, Michael cringed as he picked up the Del Monte French Style Green Beans, Campbell's Cream of Mushroom Soup, and Ocean Spray Jellied Cranberry Sauce. He got everything on the list, checked out, put the groceries in the car, and headed home.

When he pulled up to the house, he saw a thief, a porch pirate, picking up an Amazon box at the front door. Michael hopped out of the car and threw the can of cranberry sauce at the thief, hitting him in the head and knocking him out.

Michael called 911. The police and an ambulance arrived. After Michael told the officer what had happened, the officer chuckled and said, "I hate that cranberry stuff."

Michael replied, "I did, too, until just now."

Mark C. Wallfisch

Dads

"Hey, I heard you on the radio talking to your Dad, some interview, right?"

"Yeah, we've been talking, kinda resolving all those things from, you know, way back."

"Gosh, that was some mess, too. When we were kids, he was a mean pain in the butt to everybody — meaner to you than anybody."

"Yeah, can't argue with that, but we moved past that now."

"I couldn't do that with my old man."

"Your father? He wasn't so bad back then, just sorta not checked-in, not too plugged-in to what was going on."

"Yeah, that's right. But I could never get to resolving anything with him now."

"Man, if I can clear up all that stuff with my old man, anybody can clear up their stuff. You too."

"No, man, your dad was mean. Mine was indifferent."

Speeding

An EKG monitor displayed the electrical activity of the failing heart of the old man who was strapped to the cot inside the patient compartment of the speeding ambulance. The driver erratically hit the brakes, swerved, sped up, slowed down, jerked into the next lane, and ran stop signs and red lights.

The old man, along with the EMT at his side, screamed for the driver to take it easy. That sent the driver's right foot closer to the floor, sending the ambulance careening off parked cars and teetering next to an open canal.

Then came the lights and the sirens, lots of lights and sirens. They were on police cars roaring after the speeding ambulance. Another ambulance followed the police. In the air, a police helicopter tracked the vehicles below.

More officers were stationed ahead of the speeding ambulance, where they deployed spike strips to deflate the ambulance's tires, ending the chase.

Vehicles, officers, and EMTs immediately surrounded the stopped ambulance. The old man was transferred to the second ambulance, which eased away from the scene toward a nearby hospital.

While the patient was being transferred, officers with drawn weapons swarmed around the cab of the ambulance. Pointing their weapons at the driver, they ordered her out of the cab. Pupils dilated and nose running, she boldly hopped down to the street, where she was arrested.

A short time earlier, she had been walking by the old man's home, where she saw EMTs loading him into the ambulance. As the back doors were closing, she pushed the driver to the ground, jumped into the driver's seat, and hit the gas.

After she was finally stopped and surrounded, she was charged with carjacking, among other crimes.

A Reporter's Lines

Ronnie, a fledgling newspaper reporter with three days experience, had just returned to the newsroom from a grisly crime scene. He doffed his pork pie hat, hung up his plaid wool blazer, loosened his striped tie, and sat down with his notes to type his story on a manual Remington typewriter.

"The sidewalk seemed quiet, and the neighborhood appeared peaceful until shots felled a man who looked like he was in his mid-40's," Ronnie clattered away on the Remington. He continued with the story, finished it, ripped it out of the typewriter carriage with a flourish, and ran it over to the copy desk. A few minutes later, a copy editor yelled, "Ronnie!"

Ronnie returned to the copy desk, where he stood before the curmudgeonly copy editor, who chided the young man. The editor sneered, "'Seemed,' 'appeared,' 'looked like'?" Our readers want to know what was, not what something seemed or appeared or looked like.

"Did the sidewalk seem like it was quiet? Or did witnesses tell you it was actually quiet? Was the neighborhood peaceful? Dig, son. Was it peaceful or not? How old was the stiff? Was he 20 and looked like he was 45? Or was he really 45? 46? 47? Get the facts, gee whiz, and write 'em down, not what seemed or appeared or what something looked like. You understand that, son?"

Ronnie nodded uncomfortably.

"Let me put it this way, Ronnie. If you went up to a girl at a dance and told her, 'You seem to be beautiful,' would that get you anywhere?"

"No, sir, but the lines I do use don't get me anywhere either."

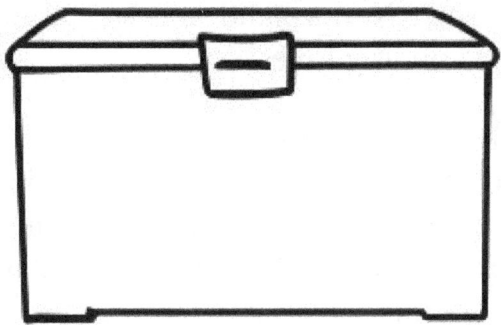

Chester's Checks

Chester's Social Security retirement benefits were direct deposited into his savings account. By the time his obituary appeared in 2012, $50,000, untouched, had accumulated in the account. Chester's husband, Neil, had his own pension, so he never needed to dip into Chester's funds.

Indeed, Neil had always said that he wouldn't need Chester's money. He had, though, often said that he would always need Chester. Every night since they had moved in together in 1970 until Neil died in 2012, he touched Chester's hand and whispered, "I can't live without you."

Every night for exactly forty years, 1970-2010, Chester grasped Neil's hand and said back, "I can't live without you, my love."

When Neil's obituary ran in 2012, Neil's sister ran Chester's obituary, too. Neil's death notice said that Neil died the day before; Chester's death notice said that Chester had died in 2010. Both obits said that they would be buried together.

Neil couldn't live without Chester, and, with the help of a large chest freezer in the basement, he never did.

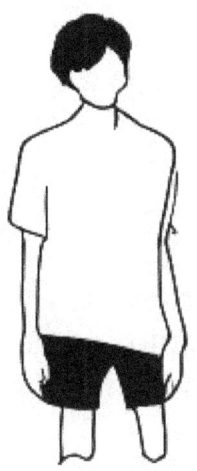

Boredom Relieved

Riley's dad worked from home, making lots of phone calls every day, not paying much attention to Riley, who was bored.

"Use your imagination, son. Do something to improve your life. You have games, apps, the whole world on the internet. What do you want to do with your time?

"I want to get outta the house."

"OK. Take a walk. Watch birds. Catch butterflies. Call a friend. Ride your bike. Go over to the lake and fish."

"Yeah, I guess."

Riley's dad was right. Relieving boredom was only a bike ride away.

Riley hopped on his bike and headed, not to the lake, but to a nearby It's Only A Dollar store. As he entered the store, Riley saw a huge array of $1 merchandise haphazardly displayed before him. He didn't want to buy any of it. That would be as boring as staying home.

So he walked the aisles with a basket, into which he put a couple of items. Several items, though, he slipped into his pockets. That was fun.

Of course, he was caught on camera and, then, caught by the store manager and, then, taken away by the police, whom the manager had called. Excitement was replacing boredom, even, or especially, after the police called Riley's dad, who, once he had taken Riley home, blew up.

"What the hell's going on? Don't you have any self-respect?"

Riley thought they must be rhetorical questions, which he had learned about in English class, so he didn't answer, which annoyed his father, who continued.

"You're not ashamed? Really? Show some ambition, some initiative, dammit. Be ambitious! You steal, and you do it at the dollar store? This improves your life? Give me a break! The dollar store?"

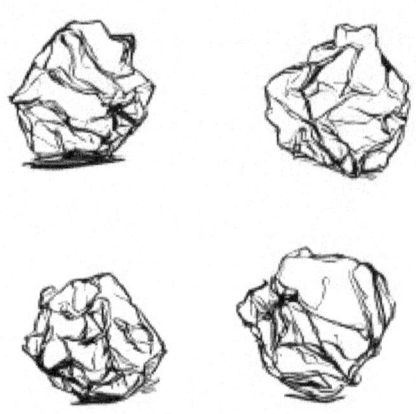

Writer's Block

Mitch grumbled to Jacob, "I can't think. It's like I'm on a precipice where I can't jump off and I can't retreat. I'm stuck. I've got writer's block."

Mitch had tried to find out how other writers got unblocked. He went online like so many others who, like Guy Noir, try to find the answers to life's persistent questions.

"You see, Jacob, I found lots of information about writer's block. I found causes, ten types, and coping strategies, practical tips, how to overcome it. Lots of famous writers have had it, F. Scott Fitzgerald, Charles Schulz, J.K. Rowling (give me a break). Damn! I really don't need all that information; I need to write again, to resume my work, to write tenaciously for long stretches. Up to now, I'd been doing great the whole time I've been a writer."

"So how long have you been writing?" Jacob asked.

"Oh, gosh, almost a whole month now."

Mark C. Wallfisch

English as a Second Language

With wavy black hair, a neatly trimmed beardstache, and light brown skin common in his native Colombia, Tomas talked with me at a stuffy reception with animated, if not perfect, English. I couldn't resist asking him out on the spot. Actually, I could have resisted, but would have kicked myself if I had. He said yes, and we made a date for the following week.

The next several days were busy at my law firm, punctuated by a very polite but careless driver's ramming her car into mine, which the insurance company totaled. Being chummy with the owner of a body shop that I refer my clients to, I arranged with him to use the insurance proceeds to repair my car instead of sending it to salvage. It had been in good condition before the wreck; I didn't need a new car.

At the appointed time later that week, I picked up Tomas in an unimpressive loaner from the body shop. Assuming, correctly, that my law practice was lucrative, Tomas expressed surprise at the "unelegante" car. I elaboratly told him the story of the wreck and the body shop. Tomas asked why I didn't just buy a new car.

I told him, "Because I'm frugal."

He quizzically replied, "Frugal? What is that?"

Flipping through my mental thesaurus, I flooded him with all the synonyms I could think of. "Thrifty, not wasteful, careful with money, economical, uh..."

Grinning, Tomas interrupted the deluge of synonyms. "Oh, you're cheap!"

His English wasn't so bad after all.

Jet Jalopy

My favorite European airline substituted a chartered plane for its own aircraft on my route from Barcelona to Stockholm. The exterior of the plane was entirely white, ghostly white, no livery at all. That was the cleanest, neatest part of the jet.

On the interior, it was a dump, like a vacation rental whose owner had taken a vacation from maintaining the place. The aircraft's upholstery was faded and ripped, the seats were unintentional buckets, grime covered most hard surfaces, lavatory doors were off their hinges, and lavatory faucets oozed acrid water.

I am alive and kicking, and able to write this little narration, because the jet jalopy did take off, fly the entire route, and land without any obvious physical injuries to anyone in the air or on the ground.

Most passengers seemed to accept the dilapidated state of the aeronautical rattletrap. The most perceptive passenger to express herself was an infant in arms. If she could have been, she would have been up in arms. She expressed what the adults were too passive to. She cried for the entire three-hour flight.

Stimulus

"With my check from Uncle Joe, I could almost buy two of these," Abigail told the salesperson at the gun store. But she said she really needed only one Ruger SR1911. It was for her car.

The ATF form at the store was easy, and the background check returned a "proceed," so Abigail was quickly on her way, nestling the new handgun into her glove compartment.

A week later, Abigail drove into the parking lot of McCoy's Mini Mart and ran in for coffee. Terry, a loiterer up to no good, casually walked over to Abigail's unlocked car, reached in, and opened the glove compartment. He smiled as he saw the Ruger, took it, and slipped it into his pocket, where it was handy to pull on an older gentleman in the neighborhood, who, the word was, had recently cashed his stimulus check.

A week after that and too embarrassed to admit that she'd let her Ruger be stolen, Abigail returned to the gun store to buy a second one "for more protection," she said. This one was for her purse, which she always carried with her.

It was the second Ruger that Abigail pressed into service a few days later to stop a robbery in progress at McCoy's Mini Mart. She was a hero. Channel 7 News broadcast a segment about Abigail called, "A Good Gal with a Gun."

The story would be incomplete without saying that the mini mart robber was Terry and his weapon was Abigail's first Ruger — and that, while Channel 7 was showing "A Good Gal with a Gun," the DA was announcing that Abigail would be prosecuted for failing to report the theft of the first Ruger.

Mark C. Wallfisch

The Impeccables

They looked luscious. The name on the plastic clamshell box declared, "Impeccable Tomatoes," and that's exactly how they looked. They looked like the tomatoes my grandmother topped with homemade mayonnaise to make sandwiches for my childhood summer picnics.

Right there, in the grocery store, standing among the apples, onions, watermelons, and bananas, gawking at the box, I saw myself stepping out of the pages of Family Circle magazine presenting a platter of these Impeccable Tomatoes to my husband and boys for dinner. My six-year-old Bobby isn't wild about tomatoes, but I wondered if he might like the Impeccables.

My enchantment continued on my drive home with the Impeccable Tomatoes nestled safely in the back of the car. I was a Walter Mitty, imagining my triumphant presentation of the tomatoes to my family.

Later, in my kitchen, I took a knife to the plump orbs. Each tomato gave a slight bounce of resistance and then burst into slices in an eruption of shades of red, yellow, and orange juices cascading out. Once assembled, my tomato platter could have been featured in a Parade magazine spread on how to wow 4th of July guests.

As I slowly carried the platter to the table like I was making an offering to the gods, young Bobby screeched, "I hate tomatoes! They taste yucky!"

"Not these," I replied. "These are 21st century tomatoes; they have absolutely no taste at all."

Insurrection

Manny, Chair of the City Council, told the Council clerk, "They're on my ass to get a resolution out right away. Draft something condemning all those guys protesting at the Capitol. They want it now."

The resolution took only a few minutes to draft and was ready for the Council meeting. It condemned "the unfortunate events in Washington, D.C., of January 6, 2021."

The Council members disagreed about the wording. They all agreed to the condemnation, but they struggled with the language. Some thought that "unfortunate events" was too polite, and some were uncomfortable with "insurrection."

After way too much discussion, Manny finally declared, "You wanna condemn it? Just call it a riot."

All agreed. The resolution passed unanimously. They moved on to consider a sewer project in Manny's district. He was angry that the project had dragged on too long.

"Sure, we're condemning the mess in Washington, but if we don't get that sewer fixed soon, we're gonna have a mess here, too."

They heard from the contractor repairing the sewer and from residents of the affected area. The Council discussed it well past the limit of most members' patience.

Manny nudged his colleagues toward a solution that they accepted late at night. He was smug reflecting on his accomplishments of the evening — the riot resolution and the sewer project.

Manny had run for City Council as a reform candidate, and he felt like he was living up to his ambition. He was dedicated to reform, to change how things are done.

Yes, he knew he was a reformer. After the meeting, he leaned back in his chair in the Council chamber, smirked, and stared at the paperweight that he, in a head-to-toe disguise, had swiped from Speaker Pelosi's office on January 6.

A Party

Lester's wife died, and Millicent's husband died. That was five years ago, when Lester and Millicent were both seventy.

A mutual friend introduced them. They recently got married in a ballroom full of family and friends.

The invitation from Lester and Millicent read, "Come to a Party. Join us for the festivities – cocktails, dinner, dancing, and a wedding ceremony. We're getting married!"

Of course, my partner and I said we'd attend, and on the designated night, we were greeted at the ballroom by a ventriloquist and a dummy, who asked us our names and told us the number of the table where we would sit. While we and the rest of the crowd were coming in and finding our assigned tables, a band played classic rock 'n' roll. A magician wandered the ballroom, pulling various objects out of guests' ears, making other objects disappear, and performing card tricks. A clown twisted balloons into animal shapes. It was, indeed, festive.

After everyone was seated, a preacher and Lester stood at the front of the room facing an aisle that had been created among the tables. The band stopped playing, the lights were dimmed, and a spotlight shone on the rear door. The room was absolutely quiet. There was no chatting, no laughter, just silence as the guests looked to the back of the room.

The guests stood up and erupted in applause and shouts of joy as Millicent, glowing in the warm spotlight, came through the door and walked down the aisle on the arm of her father.

Did He Hear That Right?

I found letters that my great-grandfather wrote to my great-grandmother while they were dating, or "courting," as they would have said. In some of the letters, he told her about conversations he had in New York with a man named William Sydney Porter, whom he described as a short, brainy ex-con who wrote stories about people in Manhattan. In one letter, my great-grandfather wrote:

"My dear one,

"It was a loud, noisy night at a tavern in Gramercy Park when I ran into Will Porter again. Trying to talk above the din of the saloon, he told me a story that he was working on about a guy and a gal who were a couple of young, married knuckleheads named Jim and Della Magi. Jim had an antique watch that he inherited, and Della had long, beautiful hair.

"Just before Christmas, Will said, Jim went shopping for combs for Della, but found the kewpie doll salesgirl at the comb shop irresistible and fell hard for her.

"Also right before Christmas, Della went shopping for a watch fob for Jim and was swept away by a smooth dude who was selling men's accessories.

"Jim and Della split and got together with their new flames but later regretted their haste. Will said he's going to call it 'The Rift of the Magis.'

"Have you ever heard anything as damfool as that?

"I'm dying to see you again,

"Yours truly,"

In the Dark

Rudy marched off into the darkness. The automated call from the power company had announced that the electricity would be restored in 3 hours. The whole neighborhood was dark. Rudy knocked next door to see if the neighbors were home huddled in the cold and dark. No one answered. Same at the second house down. He didn't know the people in the third house, but he thought he would knock. He was on an adventure, a true adventure because he didn't know what he was after.

Many times he had seen the old woman in the third house slowly gliding her ancient Ford Crown Victoria up or down the street. Rudy thought she had a husband but had never seen him.

"Why not knock? Why not knock on this third one," craved Rudy to himself. "It'll be my adventure in the darkness. I can meet the old woman; maybe she does have a husband."

Rudy knocked. "Oh, Lord!" he heard gasped from the other side of the door. Before he could indulge in his own second thought about this adventure, the door flung wide. He peered into a mostly dark living room with one pale candle dimly illuminating the scene.

"Oh, Lord! Thank you!" The old woman wailed and pointed into the room. "My husband, my husband!" There he was, an old bald chubby man balled up on the floor in front of the sofa.

Her paraplegic husband had fallen out of his wheelchair, and she couldn't lift him up by herself. Rudy lifted the old man up and settled him back in the wheelchair.

"Thank God you came," the old woman sighed.

Having had a fruitful adventure, Rudy replied, "Thank God for the darkness."

Lecture

"I'm self-taught. You guys know that."

"Yeah, Alan. You've told us so many times . . ."

"So you know I'm telling you mysteries that I've uncovered, that'll improve your lives."

"Yeah, yeah, yeah, what's the point today, Alan?"

"You know I've got no dog in this hunt; I'm just an objective observer of a world in collapse, and I've figured out how we got into this pickle."

Alan proceeded at some length to explain social, economic, historical, political, and religious origins of the current state of affairs. Each of his three associates got up at various points in the lecture to get a sandwich or pour a drink or go to the bathroom.

After a considerable display of erudition by Alan, one of the other fellows interrupted, saying, "Alan, we all appreciate your hospitality — the food, the drinks — we even understand how in-the-know you are on so many subjects. But please, in the name of Einstein, Galileo, Shakespeare, and Marie Curie, just shut up and deal."

Arthur's

"Shop at Arthur's. He'll make you look as handsome as you deserve," a well-dressed friend told me. "Middle-aged men love Arthur," he gushed. So I hurried uptown to Arthur's.

The store neatly displayed traditional men's clothing and accessories. Two dapper young men with tape measures draped over their shoulders were staffing the place. I asked for Arthur himself.

He appeared, comfortable in a sports jacket and slacks, and I told him my friend had referred me. "Referrals are the bedrock of my store," Arthur said.

I acknowledged his reputation and proceeded with my business. "I need a navy blue suit, a navy blazer, gray slacks, and khaki slacks. I'm a 42 Regular with a 36" waist and 32" inseam, though I might have put on a couple of pounds recently."

"Let's get him measured up, gentlemen," Arthur said to the tape bearers. They measured and made notes, which they handed to Arthur. Nodding, Arthur instructed them to bring a selection for me to try on.

Everything they brought looked great on me, fit perfectly. My friend's words were apt. With shirts, ties, and belts that Arthur selected, I looked as handsome as I deserved, probably more so.

I happily paid the bill, and the tape bearers took the purchases to my car.

At home, I modeled the new duds for my husband, who praised the good look. When my style show was over, my husband checked the size tags. The jackets weren't my normal size 42; they were 46's. The pants weren't my normal 36" waist; they were 40's.

Mark C. Wallfisch

Neither Arthur nor the tape bearers had mentioned the sizes to me. Like my friend had said, middle-aged men love Arthur.

Down

Hey, what's going on here? They amputated one leg years ago, and I've been getting along just fine ever since, having a great life, moving around like it took no effort. Now I can't get up. I'm on the floor. I try to stand, but I crash back down.

I'm nervous, worried, thoughts and no thoughts race through my head, mostly just worry. What's going to happen to me? I'm hyperventilating, my tongue hanging out.

Mark C. Wallfisch

Oh, god, I've got to stand up. I just have to get up on my other three legs.

One Explanation

"Your grandmother says they used to call people like us, 'The Silent Majority.' We were a big majority," Jack told his son. "Now look around. Do we look like a big majority anymore? Do they look like us?"

"Whatcha mean 'look like us'?"

"When I was your age, this was a white country. There were other people but not like there are today and like there'll be in a few years. Pretty soon, this won't be a white country anymore. We'll be outsiders in our own country, me, you, your kids."

"My teacher says that's racist, like white people think they're better than other people."

"Oh we're not any better than they are. It's just that we're on the white team, can't change that. We can't let our team lose. It's who we are. It's not racist; it's us-ist."

"What happens if our team loses?"

"Oh, my god! Everything changes. You see how we treat everybody else, don't you? Like they're inferior. We do that cuz we can. And we can because we're the majority, for now. But what happens when we're not the majority anymore?"

"I dunno."

"I'll tell you. When they're the majority, they'll treat us like we treat them now. Do you want that?"

"No, but that means we need to be nice to everybody."

The Emperor

His friends, to the extent that he had associates whose affinity for him amounted to what you and I might think of as friendship, called him The Emperor. He thought the appellation was out of respect for his poise, intellect, acumen as to sundry matters, and grace. His friends, though, felt like subjects around him, talked down to only because his consistent topic of favor was himself. His consistent topic of disfavor was anyone else.

He must have calculated the minimum interval and intensity of his acts of generosity to keep his friends his friends. He was generous enough to keep them around.

He told stories of his encounters with unappealing sorts. They were sorts who lacked appeal for him and, he urged, rightfully for all of his friends as well. The obese, the thrifty, and the ill-spoken were his regular targets of derision.

Every so often a friend would inquire of The Emperor how he viewed his own considerable weight or his own firm grip on each dollar or his own acts of belligerence toward the language. He always responded with an accurate sense of self. He would say something like, "Oh, gawd, I'm fat," or "I sure am cheap," or "I can mishmash the language up against da woist of 'em."

"So why do you tear down others for being just like you?" a friend asked.

"Fuh dere own dam good."

But Wait

"Honey, these steaks are the best. You got 'em from Montana? They're beautiful," swooned Jake over the marbled slabs of meat on the grill in the outdoor kitchen.

"I'm ready. When will they be?" asked Rita.

"Just a few more . . . Wait. Wait. What's that? What? What? Thunder?"

"It's voices, yelling. It's people."

"What the hell?" shouted Jake, who abandoned the grill and headed inside to the game room, unlocked his gun safe, and reached for an assault rifle. He paused, deciding between the AR-15 and the Bushmaster ACR that Rita had given him for his birthday. He decided on the birthday Bushmaster and pulled it out.

Meanwhile, Rita ran for her purse in the foyer closet to retrieve her 9mm Smith & Wesson pistol. She met Jake in the marbled atrium, where they could hear the rumbling outside getting louder.

"It's time, Rita," Jake pronounced solemnly. They flung open the front doors and marched down the grand staircase to the terrace below. Their mouths dropped open.

They saw hundreds of people — or was it dozens? or maybe thousands? — marching past their house toward a nearby park, shouting, banging on pots, playing music, and carrying signs about freedom, equality, peace, and justice. Jake and Rita stood frozen on their terrace pointing the weapons at the passing throng.

As the marchers saw them standing sentry, a few walked over to Jake and Rita, who ordered them to stay back, get off their property, don't come any closer, and, of course, halt!

"What the hell?" asked one of the Black marchers rhetorically. "Guys, you don't need to be fascistic. This could get outta hand."

"But wait," responded Rita, still pointing her pistol. "We're not bad guys; we like you people."

Mark C. Wallfisch

Lady Justice at Work

Maurice's swagger was obvious as he entered the courtroom. His lawyer was all business. They both took their seats.

The assistant district attorney opened by telling the jury that Maurice broke into Ms. Hattier's house at 2 a.m., found her asleep in her bedroom, and sexually assaulted her. Maurice's look of confidence faded as he listened to the gruesome account. He began shaking his right leg and drumming the fingers of his left hand on the defense table.

Ms. Hattier's roommate, a woman who lived in a separate bedroom, testified that she heard a commotion at 2 a.m. and, checking out the house, found Maurice on top of Ms. Hattier, who was struggling to break free. The roommate told the jury that she quietly picked up an antique cut-glass vase and walloped Maurice on the back of his head. He fell to the floor, bleeding and stunned. A third roommate called 911 and helped hold Maurice until police arrived.

Ms. Hattier testified last. She told the court that she was nervous to be there. She kept her eyes on the assistant district attorney. She did not look at Maurice.

Still shaking his leg and drumming his fingers, Maurice stared at Ms. Hattier, trying to rattle her. She avoided him, but his leg still shook and his fingers still drummed, and he kept staring at her. His lawyer whispered to him to sit back and calm down. He didn't.

Ms. Hattier described being awakened by Maurice forcing himself on top of her. He ripped her pajamas.

Hearing those details, Maurice froze, his leg and fingers rigid and tense.

Ms. Hattier continued, "He fumbled, trying to enter me, but he couldn't get an erection."

Maurice snapped. He shouted, "Sure I could!"

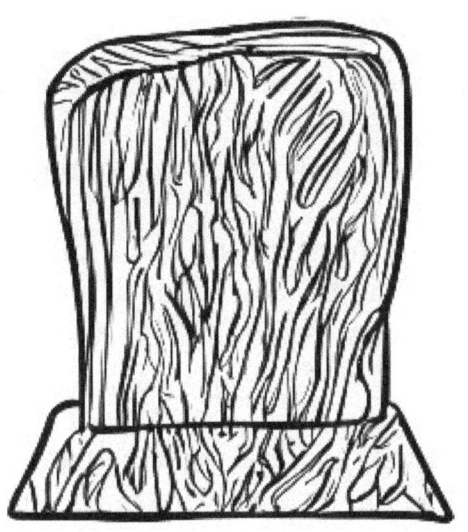

Written in Stone

On a brilliantly sunny morning of the first anniversary of her father's death, Marge, graying hair tied back against the wind, stood in front of his grave as moisture gathered in her eyes and the image of the granite was warped and distorted through her tears. Marge knew that tears are natural at this time and place, but she hadn't cried when he died or when he was buried a year ago. So Marge pondered exactly why she was crying now.

Was she crying for her father? No, she thought, he had had a long life with many joys. He had used well that body that lay in the ground beneath her, and he had used it up.

She had come to the place of that body, what remained of the physical form that her father had inhabited. But she wasn't seeking out her father.

She missed him, sure, but she didn't cry for him. She had been on her own for a year, making it, struggling, sometimes hearing his voice in her heart and mind.

What, exactly, were those tears about, she wondered. She stood and wept and turned to leave, then hesitated and faced the stone again.

Marge paused and walked around to the back of the grave to read the inscription that she had ordered etched on the reverse of the headstone. She mouthed the inscription. It reads:

He said, "Check the oil and the tires."

Then she knew why she was crying.

The Gift

A month before Christmas, Justin's girlfriend Destiny first saw a tortoise shell necklace in the window of a jewelry store at the mall. She eyed it every day walking to work at Panda Pronto in the food court.

Sometimes Justin would accompany her. On those occasions, Destiny would, after arriving at her job, slip Justin some purloined egg rolls or pilfered Kung Pao chicken, for which the impecunious Justin was always grateful.

Two days before Christmas, the owner of Panda Pronto figured out that Justin's eating the egg rolls and the chicken was eating into his profits. He terminated both Destiny's food give-away program and her employment.

Also two days before Christmas, in front of the jewelry store, a mall security guard, having been alerted by the store manager to a shoplifting in progress, gripped Justin's arm. They waited for a police officer to arrive to extract the tortoise shell necklace from Justin's pocket, extract Justin from the mall, and take him into custody.

On Christmas Eve, Justin was in the day room at the county jail. He griped about the movie on TV. "Not this one again – the wife unloads her long hair and the husband hocks his gold watch. Jeez. That's so lame."

Hermitage

"This is our hermitage, Franklin. Andrew Jackson had his in Nashville. Catherine the Great had hers in St. Petersburg. We have ours right here.

"The term comes from the word 'hermit.' Jackson's home, The Hermitage, was a retreat, a retreat from the world for him, though not so much for the hundreds of human beings he enslaved there. The museum in Russia, also The Hermitage, was built for the use of only the Tsar's family and a few others; almost everyone was excluded.

"I'm sorry you couldn't go when I went on those trips to Tennessee and then Russia. You would have had a good time.

"And now, with COVID, there's no traveling. I'm a high-risker, so I'm going to be sticking close to our hermitage for a while. You'll have to, too.

"Yes, yes, you will. Where would you go without me? There's plenty of room in the house and backyard. Down the block? You want to go down the block?

"OK, Franklin. We'll go down the block. Bring me your leash."

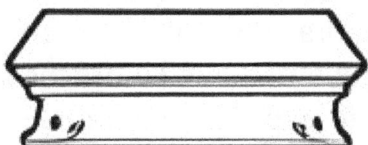

Restem in Pacem

The funeral directors had done a magical job of cosmetic reconstruction. They eliminated any sign of the hole that a 9mm bullet had made in Mrs. Abraham's forehead and any sign of her blood that had flowed from her head during a bungled robbery three days earlier. They had prepared her body for eternity with no signs of blood or injury. A frigid, dry January morning was the scheduled time for the viewing, the funeral, and the interment of Mrs. Abraham.

Donny, a neighborhood teenager, felt true remorse for letting the robbery three days ago get out of control. He had intended only to convince Mrs. Abraham to give him her cash, not to fire his pistol. He wanted to tell her he was sorry.

On the morning of the funeral, Donny donned his heavy coat to brace against the cold, dry air and trudged to the funeral home before the announced time of the viewing to express his remorse directly to Mrs. Abraham herself. He arrived to see an open casket cradling Mrs. Abraham. No one else was yet in the warm funeral chapel. It was just Mrs. Abraham and Donny.

He leaned over the casket and whispered, "I'm sorry, so sorry," as tears fell from his eyes, moistening the white blouse that Mrs. Abraham was wearing. He whispered more words of contrition and cried more tears until the heat and low humidity dried out Donny's nasal membranes to the point that his nose dripped a speck of blood onto Mrs. Abraham's white blouse. Donny pulled a chrysanthemum from a nearby floral spray to cover the blood stain, and he left the funeral home.

Mrs. Abraham then went to her rest for eternity with no sign of her blood, only Donny's.

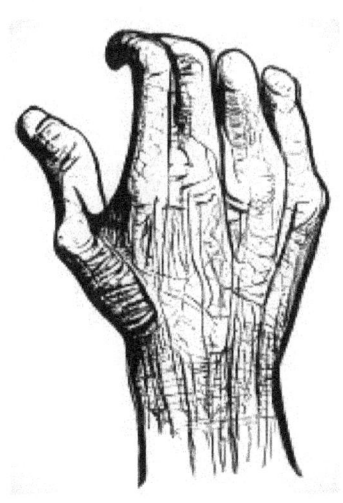

Daniel

The Bible's Book of Daniel tells us that disembodied fingers of a human hand appeared before King Belshazzar and wrote a mysterious inscription on the wall of the palace. The king could not read it. But the prophet Daniel, who was brought before the king, interpreted it for his majesty.

Daniel said that the writing on the wall declared that the king had been weighed in the balance and found wanting. His days were numbered and his reign would soon end.

Two and a half millennia later, philosopher George Santayana taught us that people who ignore history are doomed to repeat it.

Seventy-five years after Santayana's pithy teaching, an inscription appeared on the wall of the palace of a king who was infamous for his ignorance of history. This time, the writing on the wall was in ketchup.

Judging the Passengers

The flight attendant on the plane on the tarmac in Huatulco, Mexico, asked the just-boarded passengers to leave the window shades down until take-off to avoid the build-up of heat in the cabin. The vistas of the lush trees and mountains were superior to the looks of the tourists returning to the States, I concede. Even so, because I lean toward compliance with authority, I was surprised when one of my fellow travelers threw open the window shade next to her seat. Mama and Papa don't wave good-bye from the gate anymore, and the window-shade-opening passenger didn't even look out the window. She busied herself with a crossword puzzle.

After take-off, with shades and heat build-up no longer matters of concern, a traveler two rows behind me cranked up the music on his phone for his companion to enjoy and for the rest of us to endure. I had planned to ask the flight attendant to tell the music sharer to put earphones in it when the music fan figured it out on his own.

When the flight attendant came by to offer drinks, she closed an overhead bin that another passenger had fished something out of and then had left wide open.

Oh, that was yours truly. My Bad.

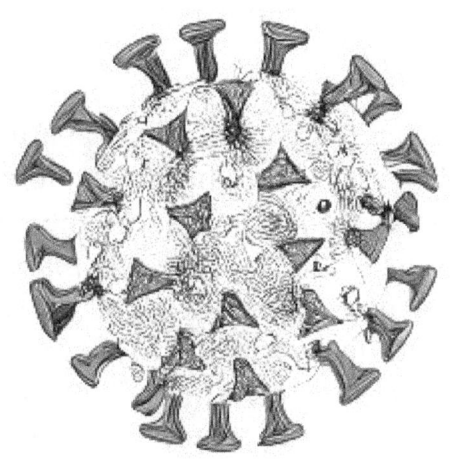

No Place to Go

It was a dark and murky apartment, home to Louis during the pandemic, after he dropped out of community college and his parents threw him out of their house, wanting him to keep his distance long before social distancing was a thing. It was a basement apartment in a house with kids running around upstairs and tiny windows looking out onto an interstate highway.

Some trucks passed by, but few cars. The governor had shut down gatherings and closed most businesses, including the company where Louis worked. Schools were empty; just about everywhere was closed. Night clubs were vacant, concerts were canceled, festivals were postponed, and theaters were dark.

The landscape outside Louis's apartment was as dreary as the interior, where the television was constantly barking news about the coronavirus, reminding Louis that there was no place for him or anyone else to go. So Louis paced, yearning to see people, to be out in a crowd. "I gotta get to people," he grimaced, not knowing if he had actually uttered the words aloud. "I'm ready to go. But no goddam place to go."

He slumped into his shabby recliner and stared away from the TV toward the floor where he had carefully laid out his AR-15 and Glock 19 next to print-outs of articles about Milwaukee, Aurora, and Sandy Hook.

"No goddam place to go."

Creative Writing

"My son is separated from his wife, who rents a room from me." That was the first line of a letter in a recent newspaper advice column.

After reading that letter in the newspaper at home, a community-college creative-writing instructor decided to assign his students to base their next short stories on that line. In class, he gave the assignment.

As the instructor explained the assignment, Gabe, a young man in the class, interrupted, "Oh my god!

That's like my father. He's harboring my deadbeat wife."

"Go on," said the instructor.

"There's nothing more to say. My father always liked my good-for-nothing wife better than me. In fact, I'm pretty sure he's been screwing her, even before I made the mistake of marrying her."

"And you said there's nothing more to say? Sounds like there's plenty more to say, plenty more for your story."

"No, nothing more to say, well, except that I'm also pretty sure my wife's new baby daughter is my half-sister."

"I'd say you've got a short story right there," added the instructor.

"Hey, that's only half a short story," another student chimed in. "I'm friends with Gabe's wife. He doesn't know it, but his older child, a boy, is his half-brother. Both his kids' father is their grandfather."

"He knows it now," concluded the instructor, "and so do the rest of you. If anybody can't get a novel, much less a short story, out of this, I've failed as a teacher."

Golden

Glimmering golden decorations on a twelve-foot Frazier fir accentuated the soaring foyer in the home of the CEO of the company where Uri worked. He was taken with the splendor of the setting and the allure of the wealth and influence of the patricians and aspiring patricians with whom he was literally rubbing elbows.

In awe of the surroundings and guests, Uri was gripping a crystal flute of champagne when Lorraine, who also worked at the company, bumped into him. "Uri! Hi! Isn't this grand? And, hey, Happy Chanukah."

"Oh my, is it Chanukah already?"

"Yeah, the second night, I think."

"Oh my, Lorraine, I've gotta go."

In moments, Uri was on the street waiting for the Uber he had just ordered. Then, arriving at a modest rowhouse, Uri let himself in with a key and called out, "Mama, Papa."

"We're in here," Uri heard from the small dining room.

In there, he found his parents having dinner of brisket and fried potatoes. After greeting them and before pulling up a chair, Uri smiled and sighed when he looked at the sideboard behind the dining table.

There it was, a tin menorah that a religious-school teacher had given him decades ago. It was 11 inches long and three inches high. It was golden color and had an image of the Ten Commandments stamped into the tin. With years of use, it was bent and warped and stained with many Chanukahs worth of soot. Its three candles were shimmering in their own light.

It was grand.

Joan

As a colleague and I walked into our building, I said, "Good Morning, Joan," to the woman at the front desk. She smiled and said, "Good Morning."

"You call people by name," my colleague said to me as we walked to the elevator. "That's good."

"I see Joan every day. If I can't be bothered to call her by name, what would that say about me?"

"I know that's a rhetorical question," my colleague responded, "but what would it, indeed, say about you?"

"It would say I don't care. And if I don't care, that makes me feel, well, crass. She's human. Acknowledging her makes me feel more human, more connected to people. It feels good, and it's not so hard to do."

My colleague told me, "I see. I get that. But do you know her name's Rita?"

"Oh. Hmm. No, I thought it was Joan. Calling her the right name would be better, but that's not the point. Recognizing her is the point. But, you know, I wonder how she'd react if I called her Rita tomorrow."

"She's probably used to 'Joan' by now."

Grampa

As a child, Stevie went to his Grampa's supermarket with his mother for her weekly shopping trips. When Grampa had the time, he'd take Stevie around the store.

On one visit, Grampa and Stevie walked up and down the aisles and stopped at the in-store bakery. "Stevie, have you met Mr. Ben? He's our new baker." Grampa introduced them. Stevie thought Mr. Ben didn't sound like he was from around there, so he asked Mr. Ben where he was from.

"Berlin, my boy. You know where that is?"

"Sure."

Grampa added that Mr. Ben is the perfect person for the bakery because so many customers ask for German chocolate cake. Mr. Ben gave Stevie a sample.

As they approached the deli department, Grampa said, "When I came in this morning, the deli was getting Swiss cheese ready. The cheesemaker was using a special drill to make the holes, and I ate the cheese she pulled out."

"Why does she make holes?"

"Swiss cheese always has holes. We gotta do it."

"Oh. OK. Mama's waiting for me now. I gotta go. Next time let's have some Swiss cheese holes."

"Sure thing. Bye-bye, Stevie." Grampa waved, and winked.

Mark C. Wallfisch

Roger Everson Thackeray, IV

Roger Everson Thackeray, IV, whom family and friends called "Rog E," or "Roggie," was educated by aphorism. Those same family and friends would proclaim to Roggie in appropriate circumstances such insights as "all that glitters is not gold," "haste makes waste," "a bird in the hand is worth two in the bush," and "don't judge a book by its cover."

It was "haste makes waste" that rang through Roggie's mind as he looked back on the mistake he made one bitter cold night six years ago. He hadn't felt like putting on all the clothes he would have needed to trudge through the slushy snow to get the prepaid cell phone he had left in his car at the end of the long driveway on his estate. He had hastily used his landline. "Goddam, haste makes waste," he kept telling himself as he sat on the top bunk of the dank cell.

If he had only taken the time to get the cell phone and not used his landline to call one of his captains out on the street, the police wouldn't have traced the call to him.

Roger Everson Thackeray, IV, was now serving ten years for trafficking in methamphetamine. Yes, haste makes waste. But also, don't judge a book by its cover.

Mark C. Wallfisch

Another Mother's Day

Miriam Goldstein, an old woman now, goes to the cemetery every Mother's Day. But her mother's body isn't there.

As best she can tell from her research, her mother's body was incinerated in 1944 at Auschwitz. Miriam has missed her terribly all these years and so much more on Mother's Day, even though, by now, natural causes would have put her mother in her grave, if she had been given the chance to have a proper grave.

But a man named Dietrich Schmidt did have a proper grave. His family gave him one when he died in 1960. On the granite stone marking his final resting place, the inscription reads, "Gone Too Soon But Not Forgotten."

"I will never forget," Miriam said as she stood before Schmidt's grave, retrieving from her pocket a newspaper article from 1960, which she had laminated years ago so she would always have it. "I haven't forgotten," she whispered.

That 1960 newspaper article reported the death of Schmidt, whom the article said was known by people in his neighborhood to have been a guard at a concentration camp before he came to the United States. The article said that he died when he was struck by a subway train on a quiet Sunday morning. No foul play was suspected.

Standing in front of Schmidt's grave, Miriam focused on the granite stone and said, "I never knew you, but I know what you and your compatriots did to my mother and my people. I remember that quiet Sunday morning in 1960 when I followed you to the subway platform. A bump, a nudge was all it took. No foul play, my ass."

Mark C. Wallfisch

Slow Burn

Billy Dwayne, twenty years old, living at home in a small town after dropping out of college, was bored. One recent night, as a palliative for his woes, he gathered his things and drove around the countryside. Recalling that he had seen the garage door of a vacant house ajar, he made his way over to it.

With a slight tug, Billy Dwayne lifted the garage door and grabbed an armful of newspapers from his car. He entered the house through the garage and made his way around, dropping three separate stacks of newspapers and quietly opening doors and windows.

He pulled from his backpack four plastic bottles of gasoline. He doused the stacks with the contents of the first three bottles. With the fourth bottle he made a trail from stack to stack and a final trail of gasoline leading to the back door. He dropped a lit cigarette on a dirty rag near the final trail before exiting into the woods behind the house.

It took a while for the dirty rag and cigarette combination to ignite the gasoline vapors. But finally yellow flames bulged out of the back door and windows, with black smoke swelling into the air. No longer bored, Billy Dwayne admired his work and left the scene a little excited.

Days later, the regional fire investigator told the chief of the local volunteer fire department that there had been three points of origin for the fire and she was certain that an ignitable liquid had been used.

"Didn't you have another suspicious fire a while back?" she asked the chief.

"Yes, ma'am, I think we've got a burner," he groaned in response.

"Yes, sir," the fire inspector agreed.

The chief turned to his deputy, his son. "What do you think, Billy Dwayne?"

Courthouse

It was a stuffy, summer day in the courthouse, and I had two appearances to make. First, I argued a motion before Judge Coleman, who had ordered me to appear in person to request a third continuance for what she called a "run-of-the-mill" slip-and-fall case. Judge Coleman was right; though the plaintiff had slipped and fallen in a grocery store, I had dragged my heels representing my client.

Second, I appeared before a different judge with a criminal defendant, who, against my advice and the overwhelming weight of the evidence, wanted to go to trial instead of pleading guilty. It was 4 o'clock in the afternoon, but the judge told the prospective jurors, "Don't worry about being kept late. This trial will take even less time than jury selection." That's when the defendant whispered to me that he had changed his mind and wanted to plead guilty. The change-of-plea hearing was short.

After that appearance, I smoothed my hand over my wrinkled seersucker suit as I headed for the elevator down to the lobby of the courthouse. I was alone in the slow, hydraulic elevator as it eased its way down from the third to the first floor.

I farted. My pungent, gaseous discharge filled the elevator.

The door opened at the first floor, and all I could say to the one person waiting to ride up was, "Oh. Hello, Judge Coleman. I didn't expect to see you again today."

Printed in the USA
CPSIA information can be obtained
at www.ICGtesting.com
CBHW021810040924
14051CB00008B/91

9 798988 740506